BED OF FEAR

BED OF FEAR

DOUG DUPERRAULT

CUTTING EDGE

ISBN-13: 978-1-962896-20-7

Published by
Cutting Edge Books
PO Box 8212
Calabasas, CA 91372
www.cuttingedgebooks.com

CHAPTER ONE

JANE MARTIN furiously jammed her hands into her slacks' pockets. Her back toward her husband, her pretty face set grimly, she glared out the bedroom window not even seeing the row of backyards stretching down the block. She angrily tossed her head to get a brunette curl out of her eye—and wished Dan would shut up. Just *shut up!*

But she knew he wouldn't. Not Dan. Not when he got on *this* kick.

"Listen," he said, "just for once, let's be calm and not get all shook up."

"Look who's calm," she hooted. "Once a week, we go through this. It always ends the same. The answer's always the same. Why don't we just drop it?"

"Maybe you don't think I'm serious about it?"

Jane turned then, meeting her husband's angry eyes. "I know you're serious, Dan. But I am too. I refuse to quit a job I like, a job that pays me good money and keeps me occupied—just to stay around the house all day."

"Don't you want a family?"

"Of course I do. And When I'm pregnant, I'll quit and be happy. But until then there just isn't any sense in my being around the house, with you gone on the road so much."

"I'm just gone two or three nights a week, usually."

"And all the days. I'd go crazy, Dan. This way, working at KLKS, I have something to occupy my time, something of my own, that keeps me busy." Now the next phase would start.

"What is there at that station that you like so much?" he asked, with the start of a sneer. "What do you get there that you don't get at home? You've got a nice house. It's costing me ninety-six bucks a month, so it should be nice. You've got a husband—" he shrugged in exasperation. "I don't figure you."

"It's just something to do, that's all." She didn't want Dan angry, but she couldn't afford to back down on this. She looked at him, a normal looking guy, his brown hair unruly from a recent shower, his features usually pleasant—now contorted with suspicion and discontent. "I like television. My work is exciting." She thought of Joe Barton, and the way he'd grabbed her the other day, running his hand up under her skirt before she knew what was happening, pinching her flesh above her stocking top and making her squeal with the hurt. It wasn't Joe that was exciting, that was sure. But she had to put up with her boss, to stay with the varied and changing world of television. "Not only that, I make good money as you know. *I want* a family, Dan, too. And when we start one, that'll be enough to keep me busy. But I'd just rattle around here now. Can't you see that?" she pleaded.

"If you won't do what I want, let's just forget it."

"Don't put it that way."

"What other way is there?"

"Everyone's entitled to something. You get to travel, selling cereal, you get to meet people. That's all I want, the same chance."

"Forget it, I said." A different look crossed his face, and he grinned. "Pull the blinds shut, Janie."

"Why?"

"Just do what I say."

"Look, honey, it's the middle of the afternoon."

"So?"

"Well—"

"Close 'em."

Jane closed the blinds.

"Now come over here." He lay on the bed, held out his arms to her.

"Dan—"

"C'mere." It was an order now, given gruffly, and she knew better than to cross him once he was aroused. Jane walked slowly to him, stood at the edge of the bed, waiting. "Take off your clothes."

Slowly, Jane complied, but only partially. She unbuttoned her blouse, then stepped out of her slacks. He grabbed her arm, pulled her down on top of him, his mouth finding hers hungrily, eagerly. His passion conveyed itself to her, and she felt herself warming in his embrace. She returned his kiss when his hands stroked her bare flesh, she closed her eyes, caressing him. As he exposed one full breast—the phone in the kitchen rang shrilly.

"Forget it," he said.

"It might be important."

"Probably a wrong number."

"I'd better answer it."

"Well, all right, dammit, but hurry."

He cursed as she got up from the bed and ran into the kitchen, her bare feet padding on the floor.

It was Alice Gordon, her neighbor.

"Jane, sorry to bother you, but when did you want Harry and me to come over tonight?"

"Hi, Alice. About eight, I thought. Then we'll have the whole evening."

"Okay. Just wanted to be sure. What are you doing?"

"Oh nothing." Jane heard Dan come up behind her. His arms slipped around her, his hands cupping her resilient flesh. "Thought I might take a nap."

"It's a good idea, when you have a chance," Alice said. "I was just baking a cake for Harry. He loves chocolate cake."

"Really?" Jane squirmed as Dan caressed her. "Well, I hope it comes out good."

"Me too. If it doesn't I don't hear the end of it for days. Is Dan like that with his food?"

"No. He's pretty easy to please, usually." Dan's lips were buried in her back, and his fingers gripped the elastic of her panties, pushing then down slowly, teasingly. Jane grabbed them with one hand, holding the phone with her other.

"You're lucky," Alice said. "Honest, that Harry! He's not easy to satisfy." Alice giggled. "In a lot of ways."

"Oh. Well, of course you'd know more about that than *I* would." Jane wished Alice would hang up. She lost her grip on her panties. Dan pushed them all the way to her ankles, then started kissing her legs.

"Yeah, I guess that's right at that."

"Look, Alice, I'll see you tonight at eight, huh?"

"Okay, Janie. Bye."

"Bye ... Dan, honest," she said with mock indignation. "Can't you wait?"

"Nope." Abruptly, he picked her up, carrying her back into the bedroom. He was very business-like now, impatient—too impatient.

"Take your time, honey," Jane said. He paid her no heed, seized her roughly. After a moment he suddenly asked, "You know what I think?"

"What?" It wasn't like him to stop for conversation.

"I think I know why you like that damned TV station so much."

"Why?"

"I think you've got a boy friend down there."

"Dan!"

"Well?"

"That's not fair. And it's not true either." She thought fleetingly of Charlie Small, the announcer. He was always hanging around her at the office, and she liked him all right. But that wasn't even like a crush. More like brother and sister. He always wanted advice about things. Just a lonely kid, she thought. And certainly Joe Barton couldn't be classed as a boyfriend. He was fresh, yes. But she didn't encourage it. "That was just mean, Dan."

"Yeah?" he said, but she could tell he was now disinterested in the subject, *any* subject right then.

"Wait," she said. "Please."

Dan didn't say anything.....

Afterward, Jane lay quietly, unfulfilled, unhappy, but not daring to say anything about it. It always angered him when she did.

He started to dress. "What time's dinner?"

"Seven," she answered, her voice listless.

"I'm going downtown and see a few people. I'll be back in time to eat."

"Harry and Alice are coming over at eight."

"Yeah. That'll be dull." When she didn't answer, he put on his coat. "I'll see ya later."

"All right."

Jane laid on the bed for a long time after Dan had left. There has to be more, she thought. Somewhere, somehow, there has to be more to life than what I've got—or what we've got together.

At twenty five, she could feel her life slipping away, and except for her work, and infrequent moments with Dan, it was all dull and repetitious and meaningless.

And nerve-shattering! Even now, when she should have been luxuriating in a glowing relaxation, she felt tense. Her nerves cried to be released from the fever-pitch they had reached during his brief love-making.

Lately, with more and more frequency, Dan left her like this—a taut bundle of raw nerves. She wondered how long she could stand it, recognizing herself as an emotional woman who needed completion....

That night, after dinner, Dan fixed them each a drink. They were relaxing, drinking, when Harry and Alice arrived.

Harry entered first. At twenty nine, he was a large, heavily-muscled, dark-haired man who ran a modeling school downtown. Always well-dressed, always jovial and outgoing, he greeted them loudly. Jane found herself uncomfortable when Harry was around. His eyes seemed hot and intent whenever he looked at her.

Alice Gordon followed him in, and Jane greeted her happily. Alice was a good friend. In contrast to Harry, his wife was plain. Jane had heard her described as 'mousy'—a quiet, sober woman who was a pleasant change from the cattiness of some of the neighborhood women. Especially Marilyn Stillwell.

"Well, Dan," Harry boomed. "Are we ready to trim the ladies' fannies in a little game of hearts?"

"We usually do," Dan agreed. With a few drinks under his belt, both before and after dinner, Dan was more amenable to company.

At the card table, Harry told the latest off-color joke he'd heard, not noticing that Alice blushed. After they'd played a few hands, Dan went to get fresh drinks.

Jane felt Harry's knee brushing against her leg under the table. She moved her leg, knowing the pressure he'd put there hadn't been an accident, getting angry as his knee followed her leg, pressing against it again. She looked at him, found him grinning pleasantly.

"Excuse me a minute." Jane got up and went into the bathroom, just for an excuse to get away from his knee. When she returned, Dan was back with the drinks.

They played for awhile, quietly, intent on their game. When their glasses were empty, Dan said:

"Hold up while I get us some more drinks."

As soon as he left the room, Harry's knee found Jane's leg again. She decided to fight it out right there. She didn't move her leg, and Harry, his face pleased, pressed his knee even harder against her.

Despite herself, Jane felt herself responding to the touch of him, found herself wondering what it would be like, if she gave in to what he so obviously wanted. For a split-second, she allowed herself to wonder what Harry might do in bed with her.

Alice got up and went to the bathroom. As she rose, Harry pulled his knee back. But as soon as Alice was gone, his knee again pressed against Jane's leg.

Jane imagined it was his hand, pressing her thigh, moving higher, higher … then broke off her daydream abruptly. Thoughts like that only led to trouble. But still, she couldn't help wondering what it would be like.

"How ya doin'?" Harry asked gently.

"All right."

"You look good tonight." His voice was soft. Jane moved consciously away from his touch.

"Thank you."

"What are you blushing for?"

"I'm mot."

Harry chuckled. "I'll tell you—"

Dan came back with the drinks then, and Jane never learned what it was he was going to tell her. Harry was a menace, she thought. Here Dan wants me to stay around the house all the time, with a neighbor like Harry. He's not exactly unattractive either, so sure of himself, so confident. No, Janie, you'd better not *ask* for trouble. And that's what you'd be doing if you were home all the time—with *him* around.

Later, Harry asked, "Say, Janie, who's that new newsman you've got down there at your station?"

"You mean George Ansel?"

"The light-haired fella with the glasses."

"That's him. Started last week. He came here from Minneapolis."

"He's all right. I watch him every night. You tell him I said so."

"I will," knowing she wouldn't. George Ansel, or any of the other announcers there would think she was stupid if she did. People outside the TV business knew so little about it. In fact, they seldom knew whether a program was film or live. The KLKS-TV Promotion Department had taken a recent survey, proving that most people didn't even know what *channel* they were watching. They watched by programs, that was all. She remembered the Promotion man's comment to her boss, Joe Barton. 'What the hell can we do, Joe? We spend money and time and effort trying to build a channel image. According to this survey, less than fifteen per cent know what channel they're watching. How can we fight that?' 'Just keep trying,' was all that Barton said.

Jane brought her thoughts back to Harry Gordon. "But that weatherman," Harry was saying, "he talks like he has his mouth full of mush. Someone ought to tell him."

"I'm sure they have," Jane said, wishing he'd change the subject.

"Maybe I should write a letter to the manager, huh?"

"I really don't think that would do any good, Harry."

"Oh? Well—"

Dan was watching her closely, jealously. Whenever she talked about her job, he felt left out. It angered him.

They broke up the game shortly. Except for Alice, they all had to be up early for the workday in the morning. After the good-nights were said, Jane cleaned the ashtrays, stacking the glasses in the sink.

Dan was in bed when she came into the room.

"What's the weatherman's name?" he asked.

"Who?"

"The weatherman. The one Harry was talking about."

"Oh. Charlie Small."

"He a nice guy?"

"He's all right."

"Good looking?"

"You've seen him on the air."

"Yeah, but you can't tell anything from that."

"He's average, I guess you'd say."

"Never mind what *I'd* say. What do *you* say?"

"Average."

"Oh."

Jane finished dressing for bed, crawled in beside her husband. She lay there hopefully for a few moments, thinking: Please, Danny, let's finish what you started earlier. But when he made no move toward her, she snuggled closer, running her hand through the thick hair of his chest.

"Dan, honey?"

He didn't answer.

"Dan, I want you. Now. I'm ready now."

When he still didn't answer, she peered closely at his face. Just as she did, a snore escaped him. Jane swore, lying there frustrated.

Dan was asleep.

CHAPTER TWO

THE NEXT morning Jane walked briskly from the but stop to the KLKS-TV building. Singularly attractive with its white, marble-ized front, it rose four stories. The ground floor housed all the offices for both the television and radio operations. On the second floor were the television studios and control rooms. On the third, radio studios and control, and on the top floor, dressing rooms and storage, an announcers' lounge and rest rooms.

She entered the lobby, flashing a smile at the receptionist, picked up the mail, and went into her office. She quickly sorted the mail, opening letters from the network and film companies, attaching the envelopes, and making a neat stack for Joe Barton's perusal. Anything that looked personal, she left sealed, making another stack. Then she checked her appointment calendar, saw there was nothing pressing as yet, and began typing some answers to viewers that Joe had dictated on Friday. There was always a flood of letters from the viewers, most of them griping.

Phyllis, the Traffic Manager, came in with the twx's that had accumulated over the weekend. There were the messages from the network, usually for Joe Barton, regarding program clearances and questions. There was also an accumulation of messages from the Reps about availabilities and commercials that Jane would refer to the sales manager.

"How's business?" she asked Phyllis. If anyone would know, it was the Traffic Department. There all the program logs were made, and the commercials scheduled. The Traffic Department was the hub of the station, all other departments spokes running from Traffic's wheel.

"Picking up," Phyllis told her. "Looks like the Fall will be good."

"I'm glad. There was a lot of talk for awhile about this being a tough season, with major advertisers pulling out or holding off."

"Well, there's still some of that. But everyone's rushing to daytime. Our daytime's just about sold out."

"Good. Maybe we'll all get a raise."

"Ha!" Phyllis said, and went on to her next stop.

Jane went back to her typing, answering the phone twice, both calls for Joe. A few minutes passed, and, without warning, hands slipped under her arms and squeezed her breasts. Jane squealed, repressing it so that no one would hear.

"Joe," she said as she turned around. "You scare me to death."

Joe Barton ran a hand through his thinning gray hair. "No offense." He grinned at her, patted her cheek playfully. "What's urgent?"

Jane handed him the mail and twx's. "You tell me."

"Okay. In a minute." Barton went into his office that lead off from Jane's. "I don't want any phone calls 'til I go through this mess."

"Yes, sir."

Fifteen minutes later, he called her into his office. "Take some messages for net, honey." Quickly, he dictated replies to the twx's that had come in on the weekend, finally reaching the last one. Then he said to Jane:

"Walk over here."

"I've got a lot to do, Mr. Barton."

"I told you to call me Joe when we were alone."

"Well—Joe." But she walked to his chair, knowing what was coming, split between dreading it and liking it. Joe Barton put his hand on her leg behind her knee, running it down over the smooth contours of her stockinged leg, then up under her skirt. Jane pushed his hand away.

"Okay," he said, grinning. "Just wanted to check."

"Satisfied?"

"For the time being."

Jane went back to her desk. Barton's freshness was annoying at times, yet it was a small price to pay for an eighty-five-dollar-a-week job, and the fun of working in television.

Barton left the office on his Monday rounds of different departments then, and Jane worked rapidly at her tasks. It was after ten when she had everything caught up, and had given the messages for transmittal to Traffic. Relaxing, she was smoking a cigarette, when Charlie Small stuck his head playfully around the corner of the door.

"Boo."

"You don't scare me."

"Shucks. Barton in?"

"No. Come on in and wait."

"I can for awhile. Got to start getting the noon weather ready pretty soon though." Charlie sat opposite Jane, smiling at her lazily. He was a good-looking blond boy. Jane liked him a lot even though, at nineteen, he was six years her junior.

"What do you want to see him about, Charlie?"

"About a raise. How's his mood?"

"When he left here, it was all right."

"Good. Haven't had a raise for six months, so I figure it's time for one. Wouldn't you?"

"I don't know. I usually take what I get and leave it there."

"Well, you're a girl. You don't have to push like a man does. You sure look pretty today."

"Thank you," she said, pleased. "You look nice too."

"Thank *you*. Say, when are you gonna break down and have a date with me? I've been askin' you almost six months now."

"I'm married, Charlie."

"So what?" he asked flippantly.

"Well," she laughed, "it might be fun, but husbands have a way of not understanding things like that."

"I'm serious, you know."

"I know you are." Her tone reflected his soberness. "I just—"

"I'm going to keep after you until you agree."

"It's very flattering," she admitted. "But I can't promise you much hope of success."

"I don't need it. I know eventually we'll have that date, sweetheart. I know it right here," and he patted his heart, semi-playfully.

The phone rang and Jane answered.

"You ready?" It was Ruth, the secretary to the assistant manager.

"Sure. Meet you in the lobby."

"What's that?" Charlie wanted to know.

"Coffee time. You wait here. I think Mr. Barton'll be back in a minute."

"You're breaking my heart, leaving."

"*C'est la vie,* my friend."

As she walked past him, Charlie grabbed her hand, held it tightly and urgently for a moment, then released it. "One of these days," he said seriously.

"See you later."

Jane, with Ruth, Phyllis, and Ann, the secretary to the Promotion Manager, had a daily coffee date at a restaurant across the street from the station. As she walked with the other women Jane thought of Charlie and felt again the pressure of his hand on hers. I hope he gets his raise she thought. C'mon Joe, be a good guy. Take care of your best-looking announcer.

They all ordered coffee and sweet rolls, and dove into the Monday morning gossip. There was always plenty of news on Monday, and always much speculation on programs, personalities and rumors. Jane seldom took an active part in the conversation, although she enjoyed hearing the others and often was able, as Joe Barton's secretary, to affirm or deny things that had the others curious.

Today, as they talked, she found herself wondering what it would be like to date Charlie, an occurrence he had been pestering her about for months. He meant it too, she thought. Being single, he doesn't worry about things like husbands. Selfish, maybe, but still appealing in a way. Wonder what he'd do if I took him up on it, or met him up on the fourth floor some day, in one of those dark little rooms, and let him kiss me? Wonder if he'd know how to act, for all his outward poise? Boy, if Dan knew what I was thinking—

"Jane?"

"What?"

"Where were *you?* Didn't you hear what we were talking about?"

"No. Sorry."

"Well, it's not important. Has Barton said anything about looking for a new Promotion Manager? Ann says Mr. August is acting a little insecure."

"Not as far as I know," Jane told them truthfully.

"Maybe you're just imagining it, Ann," Phyllis said. "As far as I know, he's doing a good job."

"Well, it's just an impression I get. I like him fine. I don't know if I could stand breaking in another boss yet. He's number three in three years. I'd just as soon see him stick around awhile."

"I'll see what I can find out," Jane told her. "But I haven't heard anything about it."

"You do that."

"Time to settle up, girls," Ruth said, and they all fished out a coin. They played King Bee for the coffee and rolls every day. The winner could get her snack free, plus a dollar sixty to spare, whereas a looser would have to pay eighty cents, the cost of the check.

They flipped their coins. Ann and Phyllis had heads, Jane and Ruth had tails.

"No dice."

They tossed again. This time Ann had a head, and all the others had tails.

"I'm King," she said happily. "I'm going to match you all."

Again they flipped. Ann had another head. Ruth turned up a head, and groaned. Phyllis had a tail, and shouted with glee at getting out free. Jane had a tail, also, and laughed.

"Well, Ruth pays," Ann said. "That's something anyway."

"*I* don't mind," Phyllis told them. "I never mind a free cup and roll."

"Me either," Jane said, glad she hadn't had to pay. Her money was getting a little thin, with payday not due until Friday.

Back at the office, Joe Barton called her in. "Take a note to accounting. Tell them to give Small a five-dollar-a-week raise, effective on his next check."

"Okay." She grinned to herself wondering what kind of luck she'd have if she asked for a raise. Probably have to undress for him every morning before he'd give it to me, she reflected. Joe pinched and felt and rubbed, but he'd never gotten serious about it. As long as he didn't, she could stand it. But if he ever really started making passes, it would be difficult. Middle aged men just don't appeal to me that way, she told herself. So I'll just forget a raise for the time being.

Although he might say: Sure, kid, starting right away.

Jane chuckled to herself. Yeah, she thought derisively. That'll be the day.

The rest of the workday passed swiftly for Jane. At mid-afternoon, she went upstairs and watched the daily children's show from Studio E, fascinated as always by the workings of the cameras, gestures of the floor manager, and the easy way the announcer, dressed as a cowboy, handled the two or three dozen children who were the studio guests, interviewing them, giving them various items of the sponsers products—ice cream, candy and toys.

Jane found live shows exciting, and watched them every chance she got.

Later, she went back to the office.

"Hey, boss, I've got a favor to ask."

"What's that?" Barton asked, between long distance calls to New York.

"Got a dinner invitation tonight. Would it be all right if I left about half an hour early?"

"What's in it for me?" he asked boldly, looking her up and down with an exaggerated leer.

Jane stuck her fanny out, and Joe patted it gently. "Okay, honey. I can't refuse you after that."

"Thanks," Jane told him. As she walked to her bus, she felt a sense of shame at the way she had acted. But, she thought there wasn't any harm done, really. Besides, it was important that she get away early.

Jane wondered what Marilyn Stillwell would wear. Nothing, if she could get away with it. And what the devil will *I* wear, she asked herself, occupying herself with the answer most of the way home.

CHAPTER THREE

"ARE YOU ready yet?" Dan asked her, coming into bedroom and standing at the window overlooking the expanses of backyards.

"Not much longer." Jane fastened the wispy sheer stockings to the rubber garters deliberately.

"Why do you dress up so much, just for a neighborhood barbeque?" Dan asked, and she wondered if she detected a note of suspicion in his voice.

"I like to look nice."

"For who?"

"You, of course. Myself. Who else?"

"There better not be a 'who else'."

"Don't worry about it."

"Just can the gab and come on, will ya? I see they're already starting over there." He stood at the window watching, and Jane slipped a petticoat over her head and stood beside him. She could see Marilyn Anderson, laughing at something Harry said, her head thrown back in gala enjoyment, her blonde hair tossing. Smoke curled from the barbeque pit. "Don't you believe me?" Dan asked impatiently.

"Of course. We'll be there in plenty of time." Jane selected a dress from her closet, put it on, and combed her hair. One lock of hair refused to stay put, and she worked with it, conscious of Dan's fidgeting. "Okay," she said at last. "I'm ready." She twirled in front of him, but he simply took her hand and pulled her along behind him.

Jane fought a desire to kick him sharply with her pointed-toe shoes. Try to look pretty, and what do I get? Hurry hurry hurry. And all so he can watch Marilyn Anderson throw herself around. He's not fooling me any. I've seen it happen too many times since we moved into this place.

They left the house by the kitchen door, walking rapidly through the backyard and across to the Gordon's. Harry greeted them loudly:

"Well, thought you kids weren't comin' for a minute. Wassa trouble—get stuck, Janie?" He laughed loudly, slapping Dan on the back and laughing again as Dan agreed with him.

"Hello," Jane said, then smiled at Alice, sitting off to the side quietly, her hair looking mousier than usual as she prepared shish-ke-bob. Stillwell Anderson was sitting by himself near Alice, and he nodded at Jane. Jane noticed he still wore his best suit from work, and wondered why he hadn't changed into slacks like the others.

Dan went into the house to get them a drink, and Jane saw Marilyn run after him to help. She forced down the jealousy she felt everytime she was near the girl. Someone had told Marilyn once that she looked a lot like Marilyn Monroe, and ever since then Marilyn had talked in a purring voice, acting kittenish and helpless. She wore tight clothes that emphasized her breasts and hips and adored the adulation of men—any man.

Dan and Marilyn came back with drinks. They stood together, sipping, and Jane looked Marilyn over carefully. She wore a transparently sheer blouse through which all could see her lacy brassiere, the creamy tops of her breasts pushing above it. Rather than a skirt she had worn slacks that hugged every curve of her body, and it was obvious to every one that she wore nothing under them.

Jane decided to ignore her blatant sex. Maybe if she did, Dan would, and everything would be all right.

Harry had gone into the house and put some records on the player, piping it through the modern music system to the backyard patio. As the first notes swam through the warm night, Marilyn put her drink down and turned to Dan, her arms out.

"Stillwell doesn't dance, Danny. How about you an' me? If Janie doesn't care," she added, making a little pout with her lips as she looked toward Jane.

"She doesn't care," Dan told her, and they moved away onto the concrete slab closer to the door.

Jane sat beside Stillwell.

"What's the good word in men's clothes?" she asked him lightly, her eyes on Dan and Marilyn.

"If there is one, I haven't heard it," he told her. "This is really a horrid drink that my frau fixed for me. One would think she wanted to get me loaded—for some reason." He glanced at Jane, who managed to grin slightly.

"Probably just slipped when she was pouring it."

"Of course."

Jane watched Dan and Marilyn dance. The girl pushed against his body tightly, so that everytime he took a step his thigh pressed between her legs. The obviousness of it disgusted her and she turned away.

"Lovely couple," Stillwell commented quietly.

Jane didn't answer him. She could have said plenty, but didn't. Could have said, Look, she's your wife, buddy. Why don't you take her in tow and keep her from climbing all over other people's husbands—like mine? Could have said, Look, don't you ever give her what she's looking for, keep her happy, keep her satisfied?

But didn't, because Marilyn's tendency to nymphomania was well known, and frequently discussed throughout the neighborhood. Whenever a housewive's coffee time slowed up, they always talked about the Johnson's who had to move away because of Marilyn, and the story of the mailman who changed his route suddenly. They were all sure they knew why, although no one could ever prove it.

Dan came back, leaving Marilyn talking to Harry, and flopped down beside Jane, taking his drink back gratefully.

"You ready for another go-round, friend husband," she asked, trying to keep it light, wanting to dance with him mainly to learn if Marilyn had had any effect on him.

"Not me. I'm pooped after one. Guess I'm gettin' to be an old man."

"Guess so."

"What do you mean by that?"

"I was just agreeing with you, you said it."

"Well, don't be so damned agreeable," he said sourly, and stalked off to the house for another drink.

Jane had long ago stopped being embarrassed when Dan acted like that with other people around. She turned to Stillwell wryly.

"Do you find me damned agreeable, friend?"

"Always."

"Thank you."

Stillwell grinned, and Jane forgot her anger.

"Come and get it," Harry called, when Alice indicated that the food was ready. They all gathered around the spit, loading their plates with hot delicious food. They sat in a semi-circle, and Jane temporarily forgot all else as she enjoyed her meal. Once she wondered if Charlie was celebrating his raise right then, wondered what he was doing.

She lit a cigarette when she was done, rubbing her leg gently where Joe Barton had pinched her that morning, thought how funny it would be if she pinched him back sometime. Maybe I will, she thought. I'd like to see his face.

Dan had moved closer to Marilyn, telling her a joke, including Stillwell only partially. When he reached the climax, Marilyn squealed and slapped his arm playfully, kicking her legs out with pleasure. Stillwell grinned slightly, returned to his food. Alice got up and went into the house, and Jane followed her in as Harry crossed to Dan.

"I heard that joke the other day, but when I heard it, the way it ended was ...."

Jane didn't hear any more, closing the door to the patio behind her.

"Hi," she said to Alice.

"Hi," Alice said, starting to wash the dishes. "Enjoy your supper?"

"Wonderful." Jane rubbed her stomach slightly to emphasize her comment. "Not starting that mess so soon?"

"Got to get them out of the way, and I'd just as soon be in here as out there. Harry's been drinkin' pretty heavy tonight," she added.

"Oh. Let me help you."

"If you want."

"Don't mind a bit."

They washed and wiped wordlessly for several moments, when Alice excused herself. "Be back in a minute."

"Okay."

Jane continued wiping, suddenly aware that someone was in the kitchen with her. She whirled, saw Harry leaning in the doorway, grinning.

"You startled me."

"Sorry. Where's Alice?"

"She'll be right back."

"While she's gone, why don't you come in the den with me? Got some new pictures of some of my models I want you to see."

"No thanks." She still remembered vividly the first—and last—time she'd accepted his invitation to his den. It had been shortly after they moved here, at a barbeque supper such as this. Once inside the den, the pictures had all been of nude girls, and as she looked, wondering why he thought she would enjoy seeing them, his arms had snaked around her waist from behind, his hands cupping her breasts, and she'd fought him for several moments before he understood she was serious about wanting to leave. Since then, he'd asked her into his den on several pretexts, but she'd always refused.

"I'll tie my hands," he offered, playfully.

"I might go in if I tied you out here," Jane told him and he laughed.

"Don't you trust me, honey?"

"Frankly—no."

"Okay," he said with an injured voice, apparent petulence. "If that's the way you want it."

Alice came back then, and Harry stood upright in the doorway. "Well," he said, "when you want a drink, holler. We've got plenty."

"I will."

Harry left.

"The good Samaritan?"

"Yeah. Wanted to fix me a drink."

"Great," Alice said, and plunged her hands into the dishwater.

Later, Jane rejoined the group in back. Alice, pleading a headache, went to bed. Jane found Dan so drunk he could barely stand, although he danced almost continually with Marilyn. Stillwell had found a magazine somewhere and was reading it, paying no attention to the others. Harry sat by the pit, drink in hand, singing to himself with the music.

Jane sat beside Stillwell, watching Dan dance with Marilyn. Marilyn was pressed against him even closer than before, and Dan's hand, behind her, dropped lower until it was resting on the top of her buttock, feeling the swaying motion of her body. Jane felt the anger rise inside.

When the dance ended, Harry stood up. "Hey," he said, his voice loud, "let's play a game or somethin.' This dancin' bit'll end it."

"What do you want to play?" Dan asked.

"I dunno. If we were kids, we could play post office," he said, his mouth in a sly grin.

"Well, we can certainly do anything *kids* can do," Marilyn told him.

Jane decided enough was enough. "We'd better go," she told Harry. "It's getting late."

"Aw, no! You don't want to leave yet?"

"We'd better." She saw Dan scowling at her, but held her ground. She knew he'd come with her—mad perhaps, but he always came when she was ready.

There was more argument, but finally she and Dan left the others and returned home, Dan stumbling over the new rose bush she'd planted the previous weekend. They didn't say a word until they were inside. Jane turned in the kitchen and waited.

"What the hell'd you do that for?" he asked, sinking into a chair, frowning. "Jus' when everything was goin' good?"

"I was tired, Dan. Have to work tomorrow, you know."

"So do I. Hell, if *you* want to come home, then come home. But don't spoil everyone else's fun doin' it."

"Would that have been so much fun? Playing post office like a bunch of little kids who don't know what they're doing?"

"Aw, it wasn't that, Jane, it was jus'—"

"Just what?"

"I dunno. You're always wantin' to leave a place when I start having a good time."

"Well, I'm going to bed."

"Yeah." He followed her into the master bedroom, flopped on the bed. Jane undressed, feeling his eyes on her but refusing to meet them. She had hung up her dress and petticoat, was unfastening her stockings when he spoke again.

"All that dressin' up do what you wanted it to?"

"Apparently not."

"You know, if you were half the woman that Marilyn is, you wouldn't need to worry about what you wore."

Jane stopped, stared at him, wondering if she should forget it. But it was too much of a blow to her pride as a woman. She stood and came to the edge of the bed, glaring down at him. "That's enough. I won't have you comparing me to that tramp."

"Marilyn's no tramp...."

"Shut up. If you wanted a damned bum for a wife, you shouldn't have married *me*. Because I'm not going to prance around and show my behind to every man in town just so you'll think you've got a hot-stuff wife." She saw he was about to say something, and knew she couldn't take anymore, so before he could say it, she said: "Shut *up!*" and turned her back on him.

She heard him get off the bed, then his hands grabbed her roughly and whirled her around until she faced him.

"Don't ever tell me to shut up."

"I will, if you need it."

His hand flashed back, but Jane didn't think he'd really slap her until the blow landed on her cheek, snapping her head back. She couldn't stop the tears then, flung herself across the bed, her head buried in her arms, letting the tears and jealousy and unhappiness flood out everything else.

"Don't ever say that," he repeated, falling beside her on the bed, and forcing her head up to look at her. But she refused to open her eyes, and eventually, he flung her head back down, and stamped around the room, undressing, muttering to himself.

Jane felt his body ease onto the bed a minute later. Her tears were gone, and only the deep, aching void of unhappiness was left. Dan got up again, turned out the light. This time when he laid down, he put his hand on her shoulders gently.

"I'm sorry, baby."

Jane waited, wanting *more* than that, more than just an apology, just a word, but knew that would be all there would be.

"It's all right. I am too."

Dan pulled her over until her body was against his, and his hands caressed her with tenderness. "Just a little too much to drink, I guess."

"Let's forget it."

"Okay." His hands moved to her brassiere, unfastening it, pulling the cups away from the full flesh, his fingers kneading. Jane lay quietly, enjoying the love play, but not wanting any more. When he reached for her girdle, she pulled away from him.

"I said I was sorry," he said, his hand still in the band of the garment.

"I know. I just don't want to, tonight."

"But *I* do," he insisted.

"You know what they say about taking two to tango?"

"Well, there's two of us."

"But I don't want to, I said."

"You'll do like I want."

"No," but even as she fought him, she knew he would have his way. She couldn't fight him, really, not the way she might have some other man, because he was her husband. When her thighs were bared, the fight was over and he knew it. His hands caressed her roughly, his lips breathing hotly on her. Jane, much as she resented it, was powerless to stop him.

Damn him, she thought, getting hot with Marilyn then coming to me. He probably just apologized so I wouldn't have any excuse. Men! One of these days something's going to happen there, then there'll be trouble. Big trouble.

"Don't just lie there," he told her. Jane moved for him. As she did, the manipulations of his hands had their effect on her, and she felt desire mounting rapidly in her body, forcing her breath to come in short gasps. Her hands pulled him to her.

"Easy," she said. When he laughed, she knew that everything was all right again, at least for awhile.

A moment later, her hands on his back dug in hard, and he yelped with the pain. Jane was glad. He'd have something to remember this night with, something *she'd* given him, and no other. For all Marilyn's sexiness, I'll bet she's a cold fish in bed, Jane thought. And then to impress on Dan that *his* wife *wasn't*, she clawed him again, bit his lip.

Later, Jane, luxuriated in the good feeling that she enjoyed with less and less frequency. If only it were *always* like this, she thought wishfully.

Only it's not. These times are seldom really good, like tonight.

She wished that Dan would now take her in his arms and tell her he loved her. But Jane knew better. It had been more than two years since he'd told her. Once she'd made the mistake of asking him.

"Don't be silly, Jane," he had told her then. "You don't have to be told, like some little kid. I married you, didn't I?"

Jane hadn't asked him again.

CHAPTER FOUR

THURSDAY WAS probably the easiest day of the week at the television studio. The rush occasioned by the deluge of Monday mail had been handled, and it was a day before the weekend frenzy would start. To Jane, it was this very frenzy, this sense of urgency and rush that made working here more enjoyable, more exciting, and more fun than any other job she'd ever known.

The others found it the same way. Barton had once tried to explain to her why worries and ulcers were worthwhile. "There's no other place, no other job, with so much split-second decision, last minute changes, and—well, I guess you'd call it excitement." He'd scratched his head as he lost himself in his train of thought. "I've tried a lot of things. Probably as many as any man. But show business, in any shape or form has always fascinated me. And this," his hand waving expansively to include the entire operation, "this is it. Television combines every element of the arts. Your commercial and promotion copy is writing, your scenic design is art in its basic form, your announcers are your actors on the stage, and the entire video picture, when it's good, is composed and constructed by the hand of the director.

"There's no other form of show business that combines all these elements. And the people," he'd gone on, engrossed, "the people are what really make it. Seldom a dull one in the lot. Oh sure, we have our problems with primadonnas, stars, kings and what have you. But for the most part they're good people, with a little more on the ball than most, a little more talent and willingness to experiment, and if they're a little more ornery, well, that's the price you have to pay." Then he'd concluded suddenly, as though embarrassed by his own oratory: "Well, anyway, that's what I think of when I think television. I hope you'll like it as much, Jane."

Jane sat at her desk, manicuring her nails. The Thursday slow-down effected all departments. The phone was quiet. There was little traffic in the hall.

"Jane," Barton's voice came through the intercom on her desk, "step in here a minute, please."

Jane picked up her stenographic notebook, straightened her seams and went into Joe's office, sitting in the chair at the right of his desk.

"Are we caught up on everything important?"

"Everything *I* know about."

"Well, that's everything then. I'm going to New York on Monday. I don't expect anything'll come up, but if it should I'll be at the usual hotel. And I'll call you every day too."

"This your regular trip to see the agencies?"

"Yeah. Twice a year, just like clockwork, ol' happy Joe Barton pokes his face in the agency doors and makes his pitch for fellowship, good fun—and business," he added heavily.

"I guess it pays off," Jane commented. "We've got a lot of business."

"I'll let you in on a secret, Janie. The reason we have a lot of business is that we've got the ratings. And having the ratings means we have the audience. If we didn't have the ratings, my friend, we wouldn't have the business, and that goes even if ol' happy Joe personally kissed—Well, these New York agency boys have their necks on the line everytime they make a buy. If they make a bad one, they have to answer for it, and after a few bad ones, all of a sudden they're not in the agency business anymore. No, they don't place business 'cause they like you. Ratings. That's all."

"Then why go to New York at all?"

Barton shrugged. "We all do it. We wine 'em and dine 'em, and they say thanks. But if you don't have the ratings, *c'est la TV*, kid. It's just something that's done, that's all. It's like voting Democratic just like your daddy did, and for that reason only. No one can explain it successfully, but lots of people do it."

"I'll bet it's fun."

"What?"

"Going to New York like that." She knew her voice betrayed her wistfulness but didn't care. To get away for awhile, new people, new places. It would be great!

"It gets pretty dull."

"You're jaded," she accused.

"Maybe."

"I sure wish I could go sometime."

"Would your husband let you?"

"That would be a case where I'd tell him, not ask him."

"All right," Barton said quietly, his eyes meeting hers squarely, boldly. "Start packing. We leave Monday morning."

"You're kidding."

"Were *you* kidding about going?"

"No."

"Well, I'm not either. So let's see if you can handle your husband as well as you brag about."

Jane sat there stunned. Was it really true? Was he serious? She could think of nothing she wanted to do *more*, right then, than go to New York with him.

"Well?" Joe asked, a slight impatience developing.

"You *are* serious, aren't you?" Still unable to believe it.

"Yes."

"Well, of *course* I'll go. I'm just as pleased as I can be, Joe."

"It's logical, honey. I need to have my secretary with me, making notes—all that *jazz*. Too bad I didn't think of it before."

"This is plenty of time," she said happily. "I—I just can't believe you mean it, but I know you do. *Thank* you."

"Don't thank me. You'll work, I promise. But you'll have some fun too."

"Oh, I know I will." She wondered if he meant what she thought he did.

"Come over here."

She did, without protest, her mind filled with the excitement of seeing New York City. She stood, quietly, while he ran his hands over her legs, then up, up higher than he'd gone before. Jane felt a tingle, pushed his hand down gently. "Please, Joe."

He shrugged. "Okay, honey. Look, on Monday morning I'll meet you at the airport at 7:30. The plane leaves at eight. An' you'd better call right now and make reservations for both of us. And at the hotel too. Get connecting singles."

"Okay." She'd had a momentary fright that he might have asked her to get a double, and she wondered if she would have agreed, just for the sake of the trip. Probably, she admitted to herself. And then she began wondering how she would explain all this to Dan.

Tell him the truth, that she'd asked to go and been accepted? No, never. I *have* to go, she thought. Barton just literally *insisted,* and besides it's a wonderful opportunity. She knew she'd have trouble with Dan's jealousy no matter how she approached it. Well, I'll worry about that tonight. Right now I'd better get those reservations made. Or no one will be going anywhere.

Early that afternoon, Charlie Small came by, after doing the noon weather.

"Can I buy you a cup?"

"Just got back from lunch, Charlie."

"So?"

I've got to tell someone, she thought. I'm so full of this wonderful news I'm about to burst. "Okay. A quick one."

"That's all I'm after, Jane—a quick one." He grinned, and Jane was surprised at his freshness.

"Well, that's all it'll be, Charlie boy."

They went out of the building and across the street to the small restaurant used by the studio employees. After Charlie ordered their coffee Jane could wait no longer.

"Guess what?"

"What—what?"

"Guess where I'm going?" she said, dragging out the delicious pleasure of finally breaking the news to someone.

"To the bathroom?"

"No, silly."

"Little Rock, Arkansas?"

"No."

"Crazy?"

"I'm going to New York."

Charlie's face sobered. "Going to New York? Not for good?"

"No. No such luck. Just for a couple of days. We leave Monday."

"Who?"

"Me and Joe Barton."

"What are you going to New York with *him* for?" Charlie's face clouded suspiciously.

Good Lord, she thought, he's like a minor edition of Dan. "He's going to see some of the agency boys, and he's taking me along to help."

"I'll bet."

"What do you mean by that?"

"I'm a big boy, Jane. I can put two and two together." He was obviously and intensely jealous, and tried to hide it by sipping his coffee.

"I could resent that, Charlie. It's not the way you're thinking, at all." She lit a cigarette, blew the smoke in his face deliberately, surprised to find that she was enjoying his discomfort.

"I hope not. You're too good for that bastard."

"How can you say that? He just gave you a raise, didn't he?"

"That was because I'd earned it, baby. Not from the goodness of his heart," Charlie said coolly, confidently.

Jane thought how great it must be to be that sure of oneself.

"Admitted. But still he did. And he's as good a guy as you'll find at the studio, Charlie. Just because he's a boss doesn't make him—what you said."

"Every boss is a bastard. They have to be. They don't have any choice in the matter at all. Except in taking pretty girls on trips with 'em," he added, watching her.

"Well, think what you will. I'm just tickled to be going, and I think it's wonderful that he's letting me go along."

"It'll cost ya," Charlie said cryptically.

"How?"

"You'll see. What does your husband think about it?"

"He doesn't know yet. But he'll understand. Probably better than you do."

"You hope."

"I know."

"Bull."

Jane fought the irritation she felt with the boy. Who the devil did he think *he* was, anyway? Yet she knew about jealousy, and, understanding how he felt about her, she softened. "It'll be all right, Charlie. Really it will."

His eyes met hers and she saw that he wanted very much to believe her.

"Really," she said again, and smiled gently. "If you like me as much as you profess, you have to believe that I'm a good girl."

"It's not that, Jane."

"What is it then?"

"It's Barton. I know his kind. Boy, get away from the home town and the sky's the limit. I'd just hate to have anything happen to you, with or without your consent."

Jane thought he was overly-dramatizing it all, but understood, and even appreciated his concern. "I can take care of myself, Charlie."

"I hope so. I guess what I really wish is that I was making the trip with you instead of him."

"Could I trust you more than Joe?"

"Well—" he started to answer, then hesitated, grinned. "Maybe not," he admitted. "In fact, I know damned well you couldn't."

"That's honest."

"I'll always be honest with you, honey." Charlie took her hand in his and squeezed it. "I'll sure miss you while you're gone."

Jane was touched. "You're sweet."

"You don't know how sweet I could be, especially on a date."

"Now, let's not start that again."

"I'm going to keep after you until you give in. You'll never regret it, either. You don't know what sweet and gentle *is* 'til you've been out with me."

"It's a shame I'll never find out," she teased.

"You will."

"You sound so serious."

"I *am* serious. One of these days you'll realize it. Then things'll be different."

"I've got to go back, Charlie."

"What's the rush?"

"Lots of things to do before Monday."

"Oh. Yeah."

They walked back, parting at the front door.

"Will I see you before you go?"

"Probably not."

"Well, have a good time." He looked longingly at her, and Jane flushed as she thought that someone might be watching them and get the wrong idea.

"I will. I'll tell you all about it when I get back."

"All?"

"All."

She tackled her afternoon's work with a vengeance, determined to clear everything away, even starting Friday's work, determined too not to think about telling Dan that night.

He won't stand in my way, she resolved. Nothing will. This is the chance of a lifetime, and I'm going to take it.

CHAPTER FIVE

LINGERING OVER the supper dishes, Jane took more time than was necessary to wash, wipe and put them away. In her mind, she cast desperately for a way to open the conversation with Dan about the trip to New York.

Whatever confidence she had expressed that day to Charlie was nowhere evident now. She dreaded facing Dan with the proposal, yet knew that she would, and soon.

He might surprise me, she thought. He might just say: Swell, hope you have a good time.

Ha!

But why am I afraid to ask him? It's not as though Joe and I were going to do anything I should be ashamed of. It's a business trip, that's all. But will Dan believe me?

Finally, despite her procrastination, the dishes were done, the sinks and table wiped clean, all the little things finished and she had no choice but to join Dan in the living room where he sat watching TV.

He sat engrossed with a Western, not moving until a commercial interrupted the story, then leaning back with annoyance until the show resumed. Jane said nothing, waiting until this particular program was over. It was one of Dan's favorites, and she knew she wouldn't have a chance of competing with it for his attention.

At length, the story concluded.

"Get me some coffee, Jane."

"Okay. But first I have something to tell you."

"Get the coffee, will ya?"

Jane hesitated only a moment. "Okay." She hadn't changed clothes and her girdle felt uncomfortably tight as she walked to the kitchen. While the coffee was perking, she went into the bedroom, slipped off her clothes and reappeared more comfortably attired in a robe. She brought Dan his cup. He grunted something that could have meant 'thanks,' and turned back to the television set.

"Dan."

"What?"

"I said I had something to tell you. Really big news, if you give me a chance."

"Oh?" He turned to her with interest. "You pregnant?"

"No. At least I don't think so. But I'm finally getting a chance to go to New York." There, she thought, it's out. The ball's in play. Now he'll have to do something with it—drop it, run with it, hit it for a homer … but it's in play.

"How's that?"

"Joe Barton—he's our manager—is going to New York for a couple of days Monday. And he told me today he wants me to go along with him." Jane waited. There'd be questions. Save some of your ammo, kid.

"Why?" Dan was scowling, and she could see the blood rise to his face.

"Well, I *am* his secretary. It's a business trip, and he'll need notes taken, things like that. I'm just thrilled to death."

"You're not going."

"Dan, there's not a thing in the world wrong with it," she pleaded. "I thought it was a wonderful break."

"He never took you before, did he?"

"No."

"So he won't take you now, that's all there is to it."

"I'm going, Dan."

"I said—no! I'm not giving my okay so my wife can go to New York and shack up with her boss. Tell him, he wants to shack up, do it on his own time."

"It's not like that at *all.*" But her protest fell on deaf ears. His eyes, his attention were back on the television. "Listen to me," she said, and he didn't bat an eye. "Dan?" Nothing. "I'm going whether you like it or not."

Jane got up and started from the room.

"Come back here," he said.

"Well, what do you know. Talking again." She felt defiant, yet afraid.

"I said you weren't going, Jane. That's final."

"You're wrong, Dan. I *am* going. And *that's* final."

She could see the anger tightening his lips, bulging in his eyes, forcing to the surface for the explosion that had to come. Yet Dan managed somehow to control it. "I'll think about it."

"Good."

"I'll let you know."

"Know what? Whether or not you decide to approve of something that I'm going to do, whether you like it or not?"

"Don't push me."

"I'm not. But this is important to me. You travel all the time. Now I want to travel. Just once. Is that so bad?"

"It'd be different if you were going alone."

"Why would it? If I'm the kind of woman you seem to be afraid I am, why wouldn't it be just the same if I went alone? You can always find someone to spend the night, if you want to, I imagine."

"You know all about it, don't you?"

"I know that much. If you couldn't trust me, you'd have known it by now."

"Besides I'm going up to Cleveland Friday night. Won't get back 'til middle of the week."

"What does that have to do with it?"

"Someone has to be here nights."

"Why?"

"Get the mail in—take care of things. It's just *out,* Jane. I'm sorry, but it's out." He had gone from anger to superciliousness. She found this hard to take—for the austere, condescending attitude was the most aggravating of his poses.

"You just go off to Cleveland thinking that then."

Dan stood looking at her. Jane was near rage herself, determined not to be denied this one chance to do something of which she'd dreamed. *She* wasn't worried about Joe Barton's effect on her honor, why should Dan, why should Charlie? She was no innocent schoolgirl, but a married woman who knew right from wrong, who'd fought off the advances of the best of them. Why, suddenly, was she incapable of doing this very same thing?

"Are you going to change your mind, Jane?"

She shook her head, not trusting herself to speak.

Dan nodded briefly, turned sharply on his heel and stalked from the house, slamming the door as hard as he could.

Well, she thought, so much for that, at least for the time being. For a few minutes she waited, expecting him to return—angry-sullen-reconciled-anything, but return. When fifteen minutes went by, she knew he wouldn't be back for awhile, and busied herself with household chores that needed doing.

After eleven o'clock, Jane started preparing herself for bed. Let him stay out all night if he wants, she told herself. This is something I can't afford to back down on. Once, just once in our life together I've got to stand up and be counted. And this is the time!

The shrill ringing of the phone echoed through the house. As she hurried to answer it, she thought, I hope he hasn't been in a wreck with the car ... I hope he's all right. She gulped.

"Hello?"

"Jane?"

"Yes?"

"Stillwell Anderson."

"Oh! How are you?"

"Let's skip the pleasantries. I'd appreciate it if you'd come over to the house and get your husband."

"What's he doing there?"

"I really don't know. Hesitate to ask, really. I just got back from a lodge meeting and found him here."

"Why don't you just tell him to go home, Stillwell?"

"Because, frankly, he's drunk, and he isn't paying attention to *me*, at all."

"Oh." She knew her voice sounded tiny, and somewhat lost. "I'll be over in a minute."

Stillwell's "Thank you" was caustic.

Jane took off her robe, drew on a pair of slacks and blouse, not bothering with underclothing, and ran over to the Andersons'. Stillwell opened the door for her, his expression cold and unfriendly.

"Where is he?" Jane asked.

"*They* are in the kitchen," she was told, and even at that moment heard a loud giggle that was Marilyn, followed by a hoarse bellow from her husband. Angered, Jane walked to the rear of the house, bursting into the kitchen through the swinging door as Dan was balancing a glass filled with water on one fingertip while Marilyn watched with fascination. Dan turned upon her entrance, and the glass and water crashed to the floor, causing Marilyn to giggle again and squeal as the water splashed on her sheer hose.

"Come on home, Danny boy," Jane said, taking his arm and tugging. He resisted, yanking himself away from her, lurching unsteadily before regaining his balance in the middle of the room.

"Get outa here," he said, his voiec slurred from drink. "G'wan New York, slut. G'wan."

"Time to go home, Dan."

"No."

"Dan," Stillwell said quietly, yet forcefully. "We want to get some sleep. You can come partyin' some other time."

Marilyn hadn't said a word, watching Jane with wide eyes, surprised at her sudden appearance. Now Dan turned to Marilyn.

"Whaddaya say, Mar'lyn? Le's have a party, you 'n me." He tilted drunkenly as he waited for her answer. Marilyn's eye caught Jane's, then she turned to her husband who was inwardly seething at Dan's suggestion.

"Danny, better not," she said at last. "Some other time, huh?" Marilyn walked up to him, put her arm around his waist and started walking him to the door, catching Jane's eye and winking. "Come on now. You 'n me'll walk up here for a minute, then you go home, okay?"

"Okay. If *you* tell me. Not them."

Weaving with the uncertain weight of the man she helped support, Marilyn guided him from the kitchen and down the hall to the front door. Jane, walking immediately behind, saw Dan's hand reach around the girl's waist and clench at her ripe breast. Though it angered her, Jane deliberately walked so as to block the sight from Stillwell who brought up the rear of their strange column. At the door, Dan leaned heavily on Marilyn, his eyelids almost closed.

Stillwell opened the door, and Jane inserted herself for Marilyn, leading Dan outside, pausing long enough at the door to turn back to the Andersons.

"I'm sorry."

"Forget it," Marilyn said, and Jane wondered how long Dan had been over there.

"He doesn't do this very often."

"Bitch," Dan mumbled, and Jane said good night, then started with him back to their house. Halfway there, he pulled away from her, walking the remainder of the way by himself, walking ahead of her and not looking back, stumbling as he climbed the stairs, then after going through the front door, trying to slam it in her face.

"Cut it out," she said, wishing he'd go to bed.

"Why'n cha leave people 'lone?"

"You're drunk." Jane started by him to the living room, but he grabbed her arm, hurting her. The smell of his breath nauseated her and she pushed him away.

"C'm'ere."

"Dan?"

He stumbled toward her, and she avoided him easily. She'd never seen him like this and she didn't like it. There was no telling what he might do, drunk as he was. Dan lunged at her again, swearing unintelligibly, and she ducked. He fell into a chair, started up again, then immediately fell asleep.

Jane watched him with her hands on her hips, controlling her agitated breathing, shaking her head slowly at the sight of him. He lay sprawled in the chair, his clothes rumpled and stained, his hair unruly, his mouth open as he drew in great gulps of air in his sleep.

Finally, she loosened his tie and shirt, removed his shoes, and propped his feet on the footrest.

"Good night, ol' drunk," she said with a degree of tenderness that surprised her. "But I'm still going to New York."

CHAPTER SIX

D AN WAS still sleeping when Jane left for work the next day and she didn't bother to awaken him. Seeing him lying in the chair where she had left him the previous night reawakened her anger at his actions, and she decided it would be better to let him wake up later.

The day at the station passed rapidly. Last minute plans for the trip were completed. Charlie came by and took her to coffee, but didn't mention the New York junket once. Joe was so busy that he just ran his hand up her leg once, which was not even par for a hungover day.

Jane went home that night with a feeling of trepidation. How would she find Dan?

Hungover and mean?

Hungover and sorry?

Hungover and sick?

Drunk?

She needn't have worried. Dan wasn't there, and she found that he had packed for his Cleveland trip. She searched the house for a note from him, but found nothing. Apparently he'd gone away mad, and this bothered her. But at the same time, the lack of a note indicated that he had accepted the fact of her going to New York—and this was worth something.

Jane ate a lonely supper, watched television for awhile, but found it didn't hold her attention. Her mind was too filled with thoughts of the trip to New York.

She undressed for bed. For a while she glanced through a magazine, but sleep soon caught up with her—and with it, dreams of New York....

The village near Jane's home had smart shops, supermarkets, gas stations, a movie house, a candy store, a health food store— and even a policeman all its own, hired by the merchants to slow traffic down and help people across the busy streets.

Jane enjoyed her trips to the village, especially that Saturday morning as she purchased items she would need for her trip to New York. But by noon she was bored, and wished it wasn't such a long time until Monday. Time dragged when Dan was out of town on a weekend. That was something children would cure. If I ever get pregnant, she thought.

Ahead, on the sidewalk, she saw Marilyn Stillwell approaching, her generous body tightly clad in slacks and sweater. Jane repressed the first feeling of joy at seeing a familiar face when she recalled Thursday night and Dan's visit to the Stillwell's. But can I honestly blame her, she wondered?

"Hi, Janie. What brings you downtown?"

"Shopping. You?"

"Same. Still gave me an extra five bucks this week, and I couldn't wait to get something with it."

"Oh?" Jane said politely.

"Yeah." Marilyn giggled stupidly in the silence that came between them. "Say listen," she said, her words coming in a rush, "I'm sorry about the other night. I hope you don't really think I had anything to do with it. There wasn't anything I could do about it He just came, and he was drunk. Well, you saw how he was, and I was a little afraid of him, really.... You don't really think—do ya? I mean—"

Jane couldn't keep from grinning. "I was just hoping you weren't annoyed with me for letting him get out and get that drunk."

"You couldn't help it any more than I could—really."

"No, I guess not," Jane admitted, and felt better. "Have you had lunch?"

"Uh uh. Thinking about it though. You?"

Jane shook her head. "Let's have it together."

"Swell."

As they ate, Jane studied Marilyn's figure carefully, particularly drawn to the lush fullness of breasts that pushed against the tight confines of her sweater. When Jane thought of it objectively, the girl's body was really amazing. And there was nothing wrong with that, not until she got off onto a movie star kick. Let's face it, Jane thought, I'm only jealous when Dan's around. But with just women, Marilyn can be all right.

"What are you going to do this after?" Marilyn asked as they finished lunch and dawdled over coffee.

"No plans."

"Why not come over to the house and we can sunbathe?"

"Well—"

"Please? We never have had a chance to visit much, you 'n me. And we *should,* being neighbors and all."

Jane found herself beginning to like the girl, more than at any other time. "Okay. It's a date." Marilyn's pleasure was obvious and genuine. Jane wondered how many female friends Marilyn had, and decided they were very few indeed.

They took a bus back from the Village, walking past the Anderson's from the bus stop. Harry Anderson was watering his yard, his muscular body clothed in shorts. When he saw them coming he laid down the hose and crossed to the sidewalk.

"Where you two been?"

"The village," Marilyn said, and Jane could have sworn she arched herself to emphasize her breasts. "Why?"

"Lookin' for you. Ol' Dan in town, Janie?"

"No," she said. "He had to go to Cleveland."

"Yeah," and his eyes traveled over her boldly. "What it was, I sent Alice to visit her mother over the weekend, and was thinking about taking a drive up to the lake this afternoon. Either of you chicks be interested in going along?"

"Well, we've already made plans," Jane started, but Marilyn interrupted. "I'd love to. Darn Stillwell, he won't buy me a car so I can go any place when he's working." Marilyn pouted at Harry, and he chucked her under the chin.

"How 'bout you, Janie? Make it a threesome?"

"I guess not."

"You've *got* to, Janie," Marilyn said urgently. "I mean, I don't know what Still would think if I went alone, but if you went—" she shrugged. "Don't you see, it'd be all right then. Please, Jane. I really would like to go."

"How about it?" Harry said, smiling happily. Jane could see no way she could refuse now. Marilyn had put her neatly into a corner, and there was no graceful way to decline. And after all, what harm would there be anyway, with two of them along with Harry? She wouldn't trust him one single bit by himself, but with Marilyn there—and the thought of the cool lake water was good.

Maybe that's just what she needed to help kill the boredom of the long weekend.

"I guess it would be all right," she said slowly.

"Good," Marilyn said, and hugged her tightly. "I'll get my suit and be ready in a minute." She fluttered her eyes at them and ran to her house, with Jane walking behind.

"I'll get the car," Harry said. "Meet me in front when y'all are ready."

Jane took her time. She took a brisk shower, then put on her bathing suit. It was purchased the year before, and had become just a bit too small—or I'm a bit too big, she thought—and she wished it covered just a little more of her creamy flesh.

Finally she shrugged. I'll be in the water most of the time, anyway. And unless I miss my guess, Marilyn will wear something that'll take the attention. It was curious. Marilyn had been just a nice gal, until Harry was there, and she had reverted to the movie-star bit immediately. Almost as though the presence of a male was enough to trigger the coyness, the cuteness and fluttering and wiggling. Jane put on a simple dress, threw a towel around her neck, kicked her feet into a pair of moccasins and decided she was ready.

Marilyn was already in Harry's car. The girl wore only a skirt, other than her suit. The top of it was a strapless bra-like cloth, in the Bikini vein, and Jane assumed what was under the skirt was more of the same.

She laughed to herself as Harry put the car in gear. And I was worried about the little bit of flesh that I'm showing. No fear, Marilyn is here, she thought, and was glad that it was Marilyn's thigh that was against Harry and not her own.

The ride to the lake was refreshing. Jane let the wind blow her hair, closing her eyes and leaning her head on the edge of the window, the wind drowning out the low hum of whatever Harry and Marilyn were saying. She was almost sorry when they arrived and the pleasant motion of the car stopped.

Harry had chosen a secluded corner of the huge lake. As he pulled off the road, weeds growing in the dirt roadbed brushed against the underside of the car, and the branches from low-hanging trees swiped at Jane's head through the open window. She could see the sparkling blue water of the lake through the pines. The car stopped before an unbroken expanse of water. There was a small sandy beach, no more than fifty feet across, completely ringed with majestic trees.

"How private can you get?" Jane asked.

"Well, no sense in going where all the people are, that's what I always say."

"How'd you find it, Harry?" Marilyn asked, obviously delighted.

"We bring models here quite a bit. 'Fact, I've never seen any-one else here. I may be the only who knows about it."

"It's pretty," Jane admitted.

They left the car and walked down to the beach, spreading Harry's robe on the sand.

"How about a beer, kids?"

"Wonderful," Marilyn said as Harry raised the trunk lid and pulled forth a cooler.

"You think of everything," Jane said dryly, and Harry laughed.

"Always prepared, yessirree." He opened a can for each of then, and Jane found the icy cold liquid refreshing and welcome. Harry sat between them, beaming at first one and then the other, his attention being gradually drawn almost exclusively to Marilyn when she dropped her skirt and sat in nothing but the Bikini suit.

I was right, Jane thought. Those pants couldn't be briefer without being obscene. And look at her stretch like that. Harry's going to forget I'm even here.

Harry was indeed fascinated by the expanse of body that greeted his eyes. When Marilyn stretched, it seemed as though her breasts would pop right through the thin cloth of her bra, and when she bent forward to pick up her beer, there was little left to the man's imagination.

"I think I'll go for a swim," Jane said, waited a moment for an answer, got none, and shrugged as she pulled her dress off. She walked to the water, the sand warm-hot under her feet, waded into the cool lake up to her waist, then took a deep breath and plunged under the rippling surface. Bobbing back to the surface, she struck out with strong, trained strokes, the water rushing by her slim body like the fast, tingling hands of a lover.

After awhile, she stopped and looked back toward shore. Harry and Marilyn were small figures, but she could still dis-tinguish them easily. She saw that Harry's hand was resting on

Marilyn's thigh, and Marilyn was leaning back on her arms, her face to the sun, apparently enjoying it.

Jane felt a twinge of jealousy. Hell, I'm every bit as much a woman as she is—probably more. But what gets 'em? The big bosom, the fluttering, the wiggling? I hope not. Why should he pay more attention to her than to me?

She knew the answer even as she thought, remembering the times he'd wanted her to come into his den, remembering the one time that she had. It wasn't that she wasn't desirable—just unavailable. Jane toyed with the thought of really fixing Marilyn's wagon, taking Harry right away from her.

That would teach her, especially after what happened Thursday night.

Slowly, Jane started back toward the shore, debating with herself. It's only for laughs, she thought. Why not? And as she swam closer, she began grinning to herself, watching Harry and Marilyn. As she came nearer, Harry took his hand from Marilyn's thigh, and Marilyn laid down on the blanket, her arms covering her eyes as though sleeping.

Jane towelled herself briefly before she too sat on the blanket.

"How's the water?" Harry asked, his eyes memorizing the glistening body of the woman, the bathing suit plastered wetly against her smooth skin.

"Nice. I could use another beer, Harry."

He opened the cooler, punched the can and gave it to her.

Jane asked, "You going in, Marilyn?"

"I think I'll just sleep."

"It feels good."

"Mmmmmm."

Jane felt anger at the girl. Why didn't she go away so she could put her plan into action? Well, two can play at that game. She noticed that Harry's eyes were roaming over Marilyn's body, and decided enough was enough.

She laid on her stomach, propped up on her elbows, sipping at her beer. "Unfasten my strap, Harry," she said, feeling guilty, yet determined to show Marilyn that she wasn't the only one who could get attention.

"Sure," he said, and his fingers nimbly loosened the material. "How about a little massage? Feel better?"

"Please."

The man's strong fingers kneaded her back muscles, and it felt wonderful. Jane glanced over at Marilyn, saw the girl watching with an expression of helplesness. Jane smiled inwardly, then put her head on her arms, and closed her eyes. The sun and Harry's fingers were taking their toll, and she felt deliciously sleepy.

"How does that feel?"

"Great."

"Harry," Marilyn said, getting up, "you want to go swimming?"

"Not right now."

"Well, *I'm* going."

"Go ahead. I'll be in a little later."

Marilyn flounced off to the water, and Jane had to repress a laugh. She heard a splash as Marilyn dove in, then only the whisper of the pines in the wind, and the hypnotic effect of Harry's fingers.

"How long's Dan gonna be out of town?"

"Few days."

"Let's get together, huh? Maybe tonight?" His mouth was close to her ear, whispering, and it sent shivers running through her.

"That wouldn't be right, Harry."

"Why not? I've had the hots for you for a long time."

"That's putting it bluntly."

"We're adults. Who are we tryin' to kid?" The fingers never slowed, never stopped, and Jane felt herself falling more and more under their spell.

"It's still wrong, Harry."

"Think about it," he said, and his fingers dropped down to the edge of her breast, pressed out by her weight, caressing it gently. Jane enjoyed it but knew she had to stop him. She'd proved her point with Marilyn. And that was all she was trying to do.

Wasn't it?

"I'd better get fastened up."

"Why? Don't you like that?"

"Move please."

Harry did as she instructed, looking annoyed. Jane pulled the fabric of her suit over her breasts, then fastened the strap in back. She grinned lazily at him, and saw the annoyed look disappear.

"Kinda crowded here," he said, almost as though it were a question.

"Yup."

"Wanna go in again?"

"All right."

They raced to the water, diving in together, and breaking up for air where Marilyn stood neck high in the water, trying to look disinterested.

"Let's do something," Marilyn said. "This is getting dull."

"Okay—you name it," agreed Harry.

"Oh, anything. I tell you what, Harry. You stand there and make a bridge, and we'll dive between your legs."

"Okay." He did as she said, and quickly Marilyn dove under, adding an extra flip with her legs to propel her. Jane watched Harry's face, and saw him start suddenly as Marilyn passed through his legs. She broke surface grinning.

"Your turn, Jane."

Jane dove neatly underwater. Harry's legs weren't as far apart as they could have been, and she knew she'd have to squeeze a little to get through. Slowly she swam toward him, pulling herself through, and as she passed under, felt him grab one buttock and give her a shove that shot her up quickly.

By the time she had her breath, Marilyn was going through the bridge again.

They did this for a few more minutes. Harry's hands became bolder every time Jane went through his legs, and once he sat on her back as she passed through, holding her tightly.

Yet Jane said nothing, sure that the same thing was happening with Marilyn, and determined that the kittenish blonde wasn't going to outdo her. Not this day!

"Who's got another idea?" Marilyn asked finally.

"Not me," Jane said hastily, hoping they'd call it a day while she still felt she had the upper hand.

"Harry?"

"Let me think."

"I'm for a beer," Jane said.

"Yeah. We can think of somethin' while we're having one," Harry agreed. Jane saw Marilyn frown, then shrug.

"Why not?"

Side by side they swam back to the beach and the beer.

"We could go back to the house and play a little poker," Harry said.

"Not me," Jane told him quickly.

"Don't know how? We can teach you."

"I know how. I'm just thinking about how it would look, if Marilyn and I were sitting around in our bathing suits playing cards with you, and Stillwell or someone walked in."

"No harm in it," Harry said.

"Come on, Jane. You're not chicken are you?" Marilyn taunted.

"Of course not."

"Well—?"

Jane was thinking. She could imagine them at Harry's house. There would have to be stakes. It would be an easy thing to make it clothes, and they'd be in a strip-poker game. It would look great if they were all in their underwear and someone came to the door. Three marriages shot to hell. Yet if she didn't agree, Marilyn would have won the day.

Well, the heck with Marilyn, she decided. Horsin' around a little here at the lake was one thing. Back in the neighborhood was something else again, and they'd only be inviting trouble.

"I don't think so."

"You *are* chicken," Marilyn said haughtily.

"Call it whatever you want. I call it good sense."

"Ha!"

"Maybe she's got something there, Marilyn," Harry said, watching Jane. "After all, like she says, what if someone came? They might not understand it was just a friendly little get-to-gether."

"Hmmmph," was all Marilyn could manage.

They went home soon after that. Marilyn had nothing more to say. They all finished the beer, then got back in the car.

Jane felt good. She'd had four beers, and her head swam with a gentle pleasant dizziness. The air rushing in the open car window was warm and clean and refreshing, and she felt wonderfully sleepy.

Harry tried to reactivate the conversation.

"What time does Still get home, Marilyn?"

"Five."

"He's going out again?"

"Why?"

"No reason. Just something to say."

"I don't know."

"Oh."

They finished the ride in silence. When Harry let them out, Marilyn hesitated a moment.

"Look, Harry. You too, Jane. I'd just as soon we forgot about going to the lake this after. I don't think Still would mind, but he's funny sometimes."

Jane saw she was worried, and felt an empathy. "Dan's pretty much the same way, so I'm with you. Harry?"

"Hell, anything you want. Although I'll tell you, you shouldn't take any shoving around from your husbands. I mean, I don't take any from Alice. I think a person should be free to do what they want to. But if you say so—" he shrugged to indicate he would go along with their wishes.

They said good-by, and Jane went hastily home, anxious to get out of the wet suit and step into a hot shower. Later, she dressed casually, not bothering with hose and the accompanying garters and constrictions, not bothering with a bra. In the warmth of early evening, she felt cool and relaxed, sipping a Tom Collins as she fixed herself a sandwich for supper.

The phone rang.

"What are you doing?" Harry's voice asked.

"Eating."

"You gonna be in tonight?"

"I don't know." Suddenly she felt fear of the man. She was alone in the house. I don't want him to come over, she thought. "I'll probably go out to a movie or something. Maybe visit some people."

"Oh." She could hear the disappointment in his voice. "Well—did you have a good time this afternoon?"

"Yes." Cooly, that was the way. "I enjoyed it."

"That's good. Maybe we'll have a chance to do it again sometime, just you and me." She could picture him, large, muscular, his eyes leering into the phone.

"Maybe."

"Yeah. Well, I'll see you then."

"Bye."

She hung up the receiver and noted that her hands were sweaty. Why? Because I know what he wants, she thought. I know what he wants, and if it had been this afternoon, I might have been tempted. But it wouldn't be any good.

Nor was the trip to the beach any good. It was stupid, she thought. What if Dan finds out? He probably will. He'd probably tan my hide for me, who's to say I wouldn't deserve it? Stupid.

Jane finished her Tom Collins, fixed another, then sank lazily into the deep living-room couch. Better watch it, girl. You'll be pie-eyed in another hour.

Evening came, and with it a cooling breeze. She tried to watch television, but was too restless to sit still. Sipping at still another drink, keeping herself at a just-right stage of mellowness, she wandered through the darkened house, wishing Dan were home.

Or that we had some kids.

*Any*thing to fill this place up a little, add some life.

She stood at her bedroom window, looking across the dark backyards that stretched down the street. The sky was filled with pinpoint stars in its black canvas, yet there was no moon.

In Harry's yard, she thought she saw a movement, shook her head to clear it.

Gone. Imagining things.

But there it was again. The figure of a man. She strained to see if it was Harry, was unable to make it out. Only that it was a man.

And he was coming toward her house, walking slowly and silently in the darkness of the night.

CHAPTER SEVEN

JANE STOOD motionless, feeling the fingers of fear crawling up her spine. She peered intently into the black night. The man would disappear into an especially dark area, then reappear again, always coming closer, silently.

He passed by her window, and she saw with relief that it *was* Harry, ending the flights of imagination that had run the gamut from burglars to rapists to—all sorts of terrible things.

Harry knocked lightly on the kitchen door, and Jane walked slowly toward it, wondering what he wanted, and knowing that she knew.

The knock came again, louder.

Jane opened the door.

"Hi."

"What do you want?"

"You alone?"

"Yes."

Harry pushed by her into the lightless kitchen. In the gloom of the room, she saw him stagger and knew he'd been drinking. As he passed her, his arm brushed against her soft breast and she pulled back quickly. He held a cup in his hand, and handed it to her.

"Came to borrow some sugar."

"Oh." She crossed to the cupboard, flicked on the light, Harry stood in the middle of the room, grinning at her. Jane filled the cup, handed it back to him, but he ignored her.

"How 'bout buyin' me a drink?"

"Well—"

"Just one. No harm in *that*."

"All right. One."

She didn't like the thought of him being there with her, just the two of them, alone, but felt that a scene was unnecessary. "What are you drinking?"

"Bourbon and water. Or anythin'. I don't really care." He flopped down on the couch, his legs sprawling out full length. "What cha been doing?"

"Nothing." Jane handed him his drink. Harry patted the couch beside him, and Jane sat there, sat on the edge of it, away from him as much as she could be. "Just thinking about getting ready to go to a show."

Harry laughed.

"What's funny?"

"Nothing. I just didn't get the impression you were going anyplace. You're not afraid of me, are ya?"

"No. Should I be?"

" 'Course not. Hell, I'm an ol' family friend, Janie." He drank deeply, grimaced and swallowed. "Man!"

"When's Alice coming back?"

"Tomorrow night. I guess. I dunno. Stay all week much as I care." Harry drained his glass. "How 'bout one more, kiddo?"

"Now, Harry, you said just one."

"One more won't hurt, huh? Be a sport."

"All right." Jane fixed herself another Collins at the same time. She was extremely nervous, and hoped it would help relax her somewhat. After all, what *was* the harm in the man having a drink or two? She sat beside him on the couch again, asked:

"How's your school coming?"

"Just great. Got plenty of homely li'l gals, wanna be models." He laughed shortly. "Funny."

"Do the girls that graduate from your school ever amount to anything?"

"A few. The one's that have it to begin with. Hell, Janie, you can't take a turnip and make an apple outa it, you know?"

"True."

"You oughta come down there," he said, and laid his hand on her thigh. "You're a pretty girl, we could help you a lot. How to stand, walk, sit—all that jazz."

"I'll bet." The warmth of his hand had penetrated her thin dress and she wished he would move it.

"I'll tell you what. I'll give you a scholarship. No money. Just come down to the classes. Whaddaya say?" He squeezed her thigh for emphasis.

"I don't think so." She moved a few inches away from him, to the corner of the couch, but he leaned closer, and his hand moved up her thigh a bit.

"Harry?" she said, and her voice carried a warning.

"Relax. Hell, the night is young."

"You've really got to be going."

"Who says?"

"I say."

Harry removed his hand. "That better?"

"Yes."

"Can I stay now?"

"You shouldn't."

"You gonna throw me out?" he asked slyly, grinning, and Jane had to smile at the thought. She wouldn't even be able to budge him, let alone anything else.

"No. Obviously not. I'm depending on you to be a gentleman."

"Always," he said, and bowed his head slightly.

"Then please leave."

"Sure. Walk me to the door."

They stood as a knock sounded at the front door.

"Who the hell is that?" Harry asked, weaving uncertainly.

"I don't know." Jane was panicked. Her first thought was to rush Harry out the back door, but if whoever was at the door had heard his voice, it would only be twice as bad. Maybe it was nothing. A package. Or something. "Stay here," she said, determined to brazen it through. She crossed to the door, opened it to find Marilyn and Stillwell standing there.

"Come on in." She saw the surprised looks as they saw Harry, surprise that Stillwell covered more quickly than Marilyn.

"Hello, Harry," Stillwell said. "Didn't know you'd be over here."

"Came over to get some sugar," Harry said, and Jane was glad he wasn't too drunk to think. "Tried to make some coffee and not an ounce of sugar in the damn house."

"Oh," Marilyn said, with a sidelong glance at her husband. Jane knew the girl didn't believe Harry, and it angered her that she should be mistrusted, incongruous as that may have been.

"We—ah—thought we'd wander over," Stillwell said, uncomfortably. "You know, Dan gone, and all. Sort of keep you company for awhile."

"I appreciate it, Still," Jane told him. "This house gets lonely when I rattle around in it all by myself."

"I imagine," Marilyn said, her smile just a little too sweet.

"Sit down. Let me fix you a drink."

Harry said, "Look, Jane—everyone. I've got to get back to my coffee. Expecting a phone call from Alice." Harry walked toward the kitchen. "Thanks for the sugar, Jane."

"Let me turn the light on for you."

"Thanks."

Out of sight of the living room, Harry turned suddenly and grabbed her by the waist. "C'mon over to the house when they leave, huh?"

"No, Harry." She whispered, hoping they wouldn't hear. Even the whispering would sound bad.

"It's all right." His hand traveled up and squeezed the full breast that was bare beneath the material of the dress. "Boy!" he muttered, grinning.

Jane pushed his hand away, propelling him to the door. "Go. Right now."

"Okay, okay." His glance went to her bosom again. "I'll see you."

"Out." She pushed him out the door, closed it. He'd forgotten his sugar. She saw the cup lying on the drain-board. Well, that was just an excuse anyway. *I just hope he has better sense than to come back after it.* She rejoined her company in the living room, found them sitting stiffly on the couch. They smiled too readily, too brightly when she entered.

"When's Dan coming back, Jane?" Stillwell asked.

"About Wednesday, Still. He has a lot of calls to make whenever he gets to Cleveland."

"I imagine."

There was a long quiet pause, then Marilyn giggled nervously.

"What's funny?" Still asked her.

"Nothing. Really. It was so quiet I guess."

Jane fixed drinks, and they sipped at them without speaking. Occasionally one or the other would try to start a conversation but it soon ran dry. Jane was too occupied trying to decipher what they were *really* thinking, and they likewise were busy with their own thoughts at what they had found—and what they concluded about it.

"Sure been a nice day," Jane said.

"Yeah," Marilyn answered too quickly. "Sure was."

"Would've been a good day for a swim," Stillwell said quietly, and Jane wondered if Marilyn had told. But a quick look at the blonde's ashen face belied it.

"If one had a car," Jane said quickly. "Taking the bus is just too much. For me, anyway."

"Me, too," Marilyn said. "I didn't tell you Jane and I had lunch together, did I?"

"No."

"Forgot, I guess. We met in the village, then we took a sun-bath all afternoon. Didn't we, Jane?"

"Yes. I think I might have got too *much* sun. I feel kind of flushed."

"It'll do that," Stillwell said. "Well, look, we thank you for the drink. We didn't come to stay, just to say Hi, drink some free liquor and go on our way. I'm about ready for bed, myself. Been a long day."

"Don't run off," Jane said as they stood to leave. "I don't have any plans." And besides, Harry might come back if you leave, she thought. Wait a while until he has time to drink himself to bed.

"We'd better go." Stillwell moved toward the door. "Thanks for the drink," he said again.

"Think nothing of it."

"Well, good night. Be good," Marilyn said, and Jane thought she detected a flash of feline hatred in the girl's eyes.

"What else?"

"See you tomorrow."

"Okay."

Jane breathed a sigh of relief when they were gone. They *couldn't* think anything wrong, they just couldn't. After all, Harry had said he was just after sugar, hadn't he? Wouldn't they believe him?

Dan wouldn't. Not for a minute. If he ever heard.

But why should he hear? There was nothing to it.

Jane went around the house, turning out the lights, locking the doors. She stood in her dark bedroom and looked over at the Andersons. There were still lights on in the house. Go to bed, Harry, she thought as she undressed. She put on a thin night-gown over her lush nudity and crawled between the sheets. The bed was cool and felt good. Her muscles were tired from swimming and she waited eagerly for sleep to come.

What a day this had been. What a week, really. What with the arguments, the excitement of the pending trip—and then today with all the damage it could do, if misconstrued.

Jane tossed restlessly in the bed. Never go to sleep, she told herself, unless you just forget everything and wait for that blessed darkness. Never mind the worries. Tomorrow is time enough for that.

She shifted her position again, bunched her pillow under her head, stretched her legs deliciously. Moonlight streamed through the bedroom windows.

Almost too much light.

Tap tap tap sounded at the window.

Jane froze. Maybe it was a tree branch. Maybe.

Tap tap tap

There it was again.

Slowly, nearly paralyzed with fear brought on by her vivid imagination, Jane raised her head and looked at the source of the tapping. She saw a man standing outside, and started violently— then with a surge of relief saw that it was only Harry.

Again.

Tap tap tap

Jane eased herself out of bed, walked to the window. She raised it a few inches, knelt down and talked through the screen.

"What do you want?"

"Forgot my sugar, honey." In the moonlight she saw him smile crookedly, weave slightly.

"No games now, Harry. Go home and go to bed before somebody sees you."

"Awww, Janie. Lemme get the sugar, will ya?"

"You know that's just a gag."

"I swear."

"Go home."

"Gotta get the sugar. I'm gonna stand here until you let me in to get it," he threatened, and Jane wondered if he would.

"Might get a little cold, a few hours from now."

"I don't care. I'll go to the front door and ring the bell— pound on it."

Jane's mind raced. It would be just like Harry with a few drinks in him, to do something like that. Just like him to bang and yell and pound and make a scene that would be the talk of the neighborhood for months to come. And coupled with what Dan already might hear, that would certainly be the clincher.

But if I let him in, then what, she thought? He'll want a drink—maybe more.

He didn't behave *too* badly before, she reminded herself, and felt again the warmth of his hand on her thigh and on her breast.

No, he didn't. But how much of that was due to Marilyn and Still coming over?

I don't know, she thought. I just don't know what to do.

"Open the door, Janie," he pleaded.

"Will you just take the sugar and go home?"

"Yes," he said quickly, eagerly.

"Promise?"

"Boy Scout honor," and chuckled.

"All right. You promised."

"Right."

Jane put on her robe over the thin nightgown, went into the kitchen and unlocked the door. Harry bounded in eagerly, grabbed her around the waist and pulled her against him, his lips seeking hers.

Jane pulled away, frightened and angry. "You promised, Harry," she reminded him, and when that had no effect, slapped his face sharply.

Harry let her go then, holding his cheek with surprise.

"Now behave," she said sternly.

"I never thought you'd do that, Janie," he said, his voice hurt.

"Your sugar's over there."

"You wouldn't sent me home without a little drink, would ya?"

"Sure I would."

"Awwww—"

"Now, Harry, it's getting late, and I want to go to bed. I've got a lot to do tomorrow."

"Well, go on to bed then, baby. Don't worry about me. I'll just make myself comfortable with a little drink or two, then g'wan home in a little bit. Huh?"

Jane was tempted to take him up on it, but something told her it wouldn't be the way he said. *"One* drink."

"That's all. Just one."

Jane shrugged imperceptibly. She'd known this would happen when she let him in. But perhaps one drink would do it, and he'd be ready then to go home and leave her alone. One thing she didn't want was a scene—of any kind. Not now.

While she mixed his drink, and one for herself, his hand rested idly on her shoulder, the fingers kneading her flesh gently.

"Here's your drink."

"Thanks, baby. Sit over here with yours."

Jane sat beside him on the couch. Harry's head was back, his eyes closed. "Getting sleepy?"

"Oh, a little."

Good, she thought to herself. The strategy was paying off.

"Sure was fun this afternoon at the lake, wasn't it?"

"Mmmm—yeah, it was all right."

He opened his eyes and looked at her. "Just all right?"

"Well—"

"Maybe there were too many people, huh? Two's comp'ny, three's a crowd?" His hand moved to her thigh, rested there innocuously.

"That's not what I meant," she said, moving away from him.

"Oh."

"Finish your drink, Harry."

"What's the rush?"

"I'm tired."

Harry set his glass down on the coffee table, shifted on the couch until he was sitting pressed against her, his arm around her shoulders. He put his feet on the table, leaned back with a sigh. "Me, too. Sure could use a nice back rub about now."

"Oh?"

"Couldn't you? Think how nice it'd feel—" and his fingers worked at her shoulders—"nice back rub, make you sleep good."

Jane thought about it for just a moment as his fingers worked insidiously. Yes, it would feel good, but not with him. *I couldn't trust him, not a bit. But it* was *relaxing.* She allowed her eyes to close. Harry's hand moved down her back, working gently at her skin, loosening the tense muscles, turning her slightly so that both his hands could do their magic on her smooth back. Jane put her drink on the floor, letting herself enjoy the massage. *It would be so easy to go to sleep now. So easy. Just close my eyes, and there I'd be.*

"Jane?"

"Mmmm?"

"Feels good, huh?"

"Yes."

"Good."

"You gotta stop though."

"Why?"

"I'm about to go to sleep."

"Don't worry about it."

"But I do."

"Wanna go in on your bed? Then you can just drop off to sleep and I'll let myself out." His voice was trembling slightly, and she heard it, yet it rang no danger bell.

"I don't think so, Harry."

"Okay." His fingers kept on, never stopping, finding new areas to relax, new muscles to loosen, and what he was doing to her back made itself felt all over her body. The warm relaxing warmth. The loose feeling, the muscles too tired to move, her eyes too heavy to open.

Then his hands left her back for an instant, slipping around and cupping her full loose breasts, his fingers working.

"Don't," she said sharply.

"Relax you."

"Don't!" She tried to sit up, but Harry pressed the weight of his muscular body against her, pinning her against the arm of the couch. She tried to kick him, as his hands continued working on her sensitive flesh, missed, and nearly fell off the couch. Her hands grabbed his, tried to pull them away from her bosom, but he held the taut globes firmly, even painfully as she renewed her grim and determined effort to get away from him.

Finally she stopped, breathing hard from her futile exertion.

"Let me up, Harry."

His mouth burrowed in her back, his lips kissing her. "You don't wanna get up, Janie honey. Relax. Enjoy it. I've wanted to hold you like this for a long time."

"It's no good."

"Shhhh."

Jane fought the tears that cried for release, tensed herself as one hand slipped down inside her nightgown, carressing her bare skin expertly. Harry's other hand swept down her thigh, pushing under the bunched robe and nightgown, fighting her resisting hands, moving higher up the smooth warm leg and thigh, fighting her tightly clenched legs.

"I'll scream," she warned, wrestling hopelessly.

"No you won't."

"What makes you so sure?"

"You don't want the neighbors coming in, finding us like this. What would they think?"

Jane knew he was right, knew that the battle would be a silent one, one that she had almost lost even now. Damn him, she thought, biting her lip as his hand reached another goal. She was tired from fighting him unsuccessfully, tired—and, despite herself, she was becoming aroused by what he was doing. His hands on her body, the weight of him so close.

I'm only human! How much of this can I stand?

Harry pulled her back roughly on the couch until her head rested on the cushion. He moved agilely and pinioned her there, one leg thrown over hers, his hands holding her down, his mouth seeking hers.

"Harry, dammit, stop!" She said, moving her head away from him, wishing she knew what to do.

"You love it and you know it."

"You're wrong!"

"Take it easy, baby. What are you afraid of?"

"I'm not afraid," she told him, trying to get through his passion, trying to make him think, and stop. "I'm not. I just don't want to do this."

As she stopped speaking, his lips found hers, holding her head with his hands, his mouth working on hers, his tongue darting into the warm moist recesses as his leg firmly held hers.

She felt herself responding to him again, and tried to overcome it, knowing if it continued he would have his way.

Seeming to sense this, he pulled her robe and gown away from one shoulder, away and down, baring one quivering breast. His lips lowered and Jane pushed weakly at his head.

I can't budge him, she thought. The more he works on me, the weaker I get.

His other hand worked up under her clothes, and the most violent twisting she could manage had no effect on him.

Jane started to cry, torn between the fear of what was happening, the fear of discovery, and the tiny voice that told her to go ahead, let it happen; for Dan would believe the worst anyway if he heard about Harry being there from Stillwell and Marilyn.

Harry paid no attention to her, enraptured with her exposed body, concentrating only on the lush flesh, the tender love spots, sensing that she was weakening under his assault.

Finally, Jane knew she could endure him no longer like this. Her body ached from her struggles, and the growing need for satisfaction, release from the torment of his caresses. And what would be the harm? she asked herself. What's the difference between having Dan angry for an imagined injustice, or having him angry for an actual one? What was the damned difference?

"Harry."

"Shut up."

"Harry!"

"What?"

"Turn out the light."

He smiled then, sensuously, happily, knowing he had won. He got up quickly, crossed to the lamp and flicked it out. In the moonlight that filtered into the room, Jane saw him taking off his clothes, and for a moment panicked.

What am I doing? What am I doing?

She started to get up from the couch, but he was beside her, pushing her back, kissing her deeply, his hands busy.

"Let's go in on the bed," he whispered.

"No."

"Why not?"

"No."

"Okay." He pulled her robe off, flung it to the floor, then raised her gown.

"Harry?"

"What?" Impatiently.

"Take your time, please."

"Okay," he said shortly, pulling her gown up and over her head, looking at her nude body for a long moment, then catching her roughly and forcing her back on the couch.

"You're heavy."

"Mmmm."

"Take your *time!*"

"Oh, baby—oh, baby."

"Slow down," she pleaded, but his ears were deaf to her request.

Jane fought to match him, but there was only haste on his part—haste for the gratification he had wanted so long. Her pleadings were lost on him, he was totally unaware that she was even speaking to him.

Finally, he gasped gutterally, collapsing as she said, "Not yet, not yet."

But it was too late.

"You bastard," she said bitterly.

"Honey, I couldn't help it."

"You didn't try."

"Janie—"

"Get out of here."

"Honey—"

"Get *out!* You got what you came for. Now get *out!*"

Slowly, Harry got up from the couch. "Okay, okay."

"Hurry."

She watched him dress, hating him, hating herself. Her body was torn with frustrated desire, aching all over.

"Look, Janie—"

"Just go. Don't say another damned word. Get out!"

"You're the boss."

She watched him leave the room, heard the kitchen door open and shut, and only then allowed herself the release of the tears that were welling within her.

She'd gambled and lost, and the defeat was painful.

All she'd accomplished was to add to her guilt—with nothing to qualify it, nothing to remember pleasantly.

I just hope he can keep his mouth shut, she thought. I just hope he doesn't get drunk some night and start getting smart, hinting around and being sly and giving everything away.

He got what he wanted, why should he?

But she knew his type, and feared him.

And Dan—what about him, when he came home and heard that Harry had been over there? What about the accusations that would follow? Would she be able to lie successfully, after what had happened?

I'd better, she told herself. I'd damn well better.

After a bath, she didn't feel any improvement, and finally downed a double shot to help her to relax.

I can't face him again, she thought, thinking of Harry. I couldn't look him in the eye. But she knew she would have to, probably many times, and it frightened her.

Why did I do it? Why did I give in to him? If only I'd never let him in to begin with, this wouldn't have happened. I'd be sleeping without a care in the world.

This thought brought more tears, tears of self-pity, and while she was crying bitterly over her mistake, an uneasy sleep finally came to her.

CHAPTER EIGHT

O N MONDAY morning, Jane arrived at the airport fifteen minutes before Joe Barton, waiting nervously for him to come as the time of their plane's departure neared.

Sunday she had spent packing. Several times the phone had rung shrilly, but she had ignored it, fearing it would be Harry and not wanting to talk to him, think about him, or see him. She wanted to remember Saturday night as a bad dream, a nightmare from which she could awaken, never having to tell anyone about her dream. She had retired early and slept deeply, her alarm clock jangling her awake at five o'clock.

She glanced up at the row of clocks on the wall of the terminal, saw by the largest (local time) that there was only fifteen minutes until flight time. Ranged beside the clock were smaller ones giving the times in London, Berlin, Tokyo, Hawaii.

C'mon, Joe, she thought impatiently, her eyes sweeping the busy place, searching—then seeing him coming through the front doors, waving to him eagerly with building excitement.

Barton indicated she should follow him and led her to the counter of the particular airline they were using, helped her put her bag on the scales, confirmed their reservations, then took her arm as he led her outside to the flight line, speaking for the first time.

"Think I wasn't gonna make it?"

"I was beginning to worry," she admitted.

"Me, too. I couldn't start my damned car and had to get the garage guy to come." His eyes swept over her appraisingly. "You look great. You'll set these agency guys on their ears."

"I hope so. I want to be of some use to you, besides company."

"Don't worry," he said cryptically. "You will."

Their flight was waiting at Gate 12. Jane tingled with anticipation as she preceded Joe up the narrow stairs to the plane itself, letting him select the seats.

"Good idea to sit well forward," he said, letting her have the window seat. "Get less vibration that way."

Jane looked outside through the small aperture. Her seat was just in front of the port engines and she knew she would be able to see everything, once they were aloft. She turned, smiling, to Joe.

"You may have already guessed it, but I've never flown before."

"I had a hunch. But there's nothing to worry about." He checked his watch. "We have about five minutes 'til take-off. You might as well fix your safety belt, smoke, and relax."

"Okay." She did as he directed and was just taking her last puff of the cigarette when the words "No Smoking" lit up on the sign at the front of the cabin. The plane's engines turned, coughed, then roared to life, and soon the plane was taxi-ing out to the runway, bouncing gently along the cement strip. Jane felt herself tensing. Barton noticed it and took her hand in his.

"We'll pause a minute before we take off," he told her quietly. "The pilot makes a last check of all his instruments. When he gets clearance, we'll be off. The pressure will push you back in your seat for a few seconds, then things will get a lot quieter, and we'll be in the air."

Jane found it was exactly as he said. While the plane waited for clearance, there was a click, and a woman's voice came over the loudspeaker.

"This is your stewardess, Mary Fisher. Welcome aboard Flight 827, non-stop to New York City. We will fly at an altitude of 6,000 feet and we are scheduled to arrive at 9:12. Your pilot is Roy Irving. Please fasten your seat belts. Thank you."

Jane clung to Joe's hand as the plane roared down the runway, then lifted easily into the air. Fascinated, she watched the ground below fall away, saw the familiar houses and cars and trees and roads become smaller and smaller until they were like a tiny doll-world. The plane went higher, into and through some clouds, then above them. Jane eased her hand out of Joe's grasp.

"Amazing," she murmured.

"Quite an experience, the first time."

"Oh, it's wonderful. Already it's like a different world."

Barton leaned closer to her, and she saw his eyes drop to her bulging breasts. "This whole trip'll be like that for you, honey. Completely different from anything you've known, all new, all fun."

"I hope so."

"It will."

The flight didn't last long enough for Jane. Long before she was ready for it to end they had arrived at LaGuardia Field, then the rush to get their bags, the rush to the limousine, the ride into New York too fast for her to absorb all the things she had waited so long to see.

Only when they had checked into their hotel did she feel at all relaxed, but even that was temporary, as Joe pointed out.

He came into her room from the connecting door unannounced as she was fixing her stockings, watching her wordlessly as she fastened her garters again, then pulled her skirt down, conscious of the thoughts that must be running through his head.

"How about a drink before we make the first call?"

"Oh Joe, it's too early for me. It's not even ten-thirty."

Barton shrugged, walked close to her, inspecting her, taking her shoulder and turning her around. Then he patted her buttock lightly. "You look fine, kid. Let's get started."

"Okay."

"You know, on second thought, these agencies I'm going to see today are mainly social calls. I don't imagine there'll be much of a business nature."

"Oh?"

"Why don't you just take the day and see what you want to, go to a show, do some shopping, you know?"

"But I want to help, Joe. If I can."

"Now, you just enjoy yourself. Have fun, and I'll meet you back here about six."

"But—will that be all right?" She had expected to be by his side during the trips to agency and network offices, to see at first hand the mechanics of the trip. She couldn't help but feel a certain disappointment, even though the prospect of a whole day by herself in New York appealed to her.

"Sure. To be honest, the main reason I brought you along was to give you a chance to have a little vacation on the company. You've earned it."

"If you're sure—"

"Don't worry, it's all right." He patted her again. "Just be back by six. I'll meet you right here."

"Okay, Joe. And thanks."

As he left, she realized that he hadn't ever really needed her help on the trip, as he had professed back home.

I wonder if I really believed it, at all, she asked herself, or was I kidding myself? Maybe Charlie was right after all.

She shrugged, determined not to think about it. She had an entire day in a glamorous city, and what could be better than that?

It was a day that passed quickly. She took a sightseeing bus ride, ate at an Automat, rode a ferry to Staten Island, went to the top of the Empire State Building, and ended up, late in the afternoon, in Central Park, tired but very happy. She had memories that, but for Joe Barton, she might never have had. She ran the events of the day through her mind again and again, imagining the pleasure she would derive from relating them to Dan—then remembering the way they had parted, recalling for the first time the problems that awaited her at home:

Damn, she thought.

But at least I have another day—and a night—here before any of that. And I'm going to enjoy it too, dammit.

She realized it was getting late, and took a taxi to the hotel, hastening into the shower before Joe returned, dressing carefully in a black cocktail dress with a daringly low-cut bodice, a dress that Dan had forbidden her to wear when he had seen it, more than a year ago, but one she had kept, awaiting a chance to use it, loving it despite his objections.

It was cut too low to allow any form of brassiere, and what support there was for her breasts was built into the dress itself. The material extended only about an inch above her crests, and she knew that Barton's eyes would pop when he saw her. When she was dressed, she ordered ice and mixer from Room Service.

When Barton entered his room at a few minutes after six, she was waiting for him, a cold highball extended toward him with a grin.

His mouth dropped open at the sight of her, and she felt deep pride in her womanliness, thrusting her bosom out slightly as he accepted the drink with a grateful sigh, sitting on the edge of his bed.

"You are a knockout," he announced, after taking a long drink of his highball.

Jane curtseyed, picking up her own drink, and sitting carefully in a chair. "Thank you. I was hoping you'd be pleased."

"That's not the word, honey."

"How was your day?"

"Huh?" His thoughts had obviously been on things more mundane, and she laughed, repeating her question. "Oh, not bad. Things look real good for the fall, if we can keep our numbers up. Probably better than last year. More advertisers getting into TV. How about another drink?"

"I'm at your command," she said, feeling daring, knowing he would take her words suggestively, and not caring. She handed him a fresh drink and as he took it with one hand, he beckoned her closer with the other.

Jane braced herself, walked forward until she was standing between his legs. Joe's arm went around her buttocks, pulling her soft belly against his face, pressing his lips against her dress, then pulling her over gently until her breasts were level with his face, kissing the deep cleavage, his mouth soft on her skin.

Jane felt herself tremble, extricated herself slowly. She drank deeply, and when he smiled slowly, she knew he understood more than she wanted him to.

Just the small amount of contact they had had—just that much had brought her nerves to screaming wakefullness, nerves that Dan—and Harry, oh, yes Harry—had rubbed raw. She drank to overcome it, knowing that liquor alone would never be the answer.

Barton stood up and stretched. "I'll be ready in a minute and we'll have supper. There's a good steak house a coupla blocks away."

He went into the bathroom, and she wondered if he was teasing her. It must have been obvious to him, her need, her crying desperate intense physical need. A man like Joe would sense that. Wouldn't he?

Jane had finished her drink when he came back into the room. She was relaxing with the influence of the alcohol, and realized suddenly that she was ravenous.

"All set?" he asked.

"Yes. I'm starved to death."

"Good. Even when it's on the arm, it's better if you really enjoy it."

"On the arm?"

"Expense account."

"Oh."

At the door, he pulled her to him and she found her body complying, fitting itself against him. He kissed her ear, then bent his lips to her breast.

"Joe—" she said, the nerves starting again.

"Okay," he said, and followed her into the corridor.

The steaks were as good as he had promised. Afterward, he had a surprise for her. Two tickets for the top musical in town that he had obtained somehow during the day.

As she sat beside him in the theatre, Jane found it hard to imagine that the Joe Barton beside her was the same boss that she worked for at KLKS. He was so different from the pinching, feeling, patting Barton—or was he? Had she not perhaps misjudged, mis-guessed about him?

She didn't know. All she was sure of was that she had spent a wonderful day, the evening was great, and she sensed it was leading to a climax later that had been predictable when the plans for the trip had begun, a climax that she found herself even looking forward to, not fearing as she would have imagined.

After the show, he took her to the Copa where they saw the late show, drinking enough to restore the pleasant alcoholic glow that she found so relaxing.

They went to another place after that, a more intimate, darker room, where they danced. Jane's pleasure as their bodies swayed together would have frightened her, had she not had the reassurance of the drinks. When they returned to their table, Joe's hand slipped under her dress, between her legs, and involuntarily, she pressed her knees together imprisoning his hand.

Her eyes met his, and he saw the pain in them.

"Let's go."

Jane nodded, wishing it didn't take so long to pay the check, to find a cab, to reach the hotel, to get upstairs.

Inside his room he grabbed her roughly, pushing her toward the bed.

"Let me take my dress off."

"All right."

He watched her as she unzipped her dress, pulled it over her head. She stood before him proudly, knowing the jutting breasts, molded hips and thighs were as good or better than any he had ever known. Barton watched her rapturously as she unfastened her stockings, then walked toward the light.

"Don't!"

"Why?"

"I want to see you."

"Later."

Jane flicked the switch, plunging the room into darkness. Then she wriggled out of her girdle, peeling her stockings off. She heard a rustling and knew he was undressing too. Slowly she walked toward the bed, guided to him by his breathing, reaching out until she touched him.

He pulled her tightly against him. His mouth found hers as they fell together on the bed. His love was rough and urgent and she returned his caresses in kind, eagerly.

They hurried, spending little time with preliminaries, neither desirous of any wasted time. Their joining was painless, fulfilling, and Jane thought she would burst.

Quickly, they went together down what could have been an old familiar road, until they came to the top of the hill and the sunlight over the ridge burst in their faces, blinding them with its intensity.

"Sonuvabitch," Joe said, squeezing her to him.

"Brother!" she answered, tears welling in her eyes from the joy, the completeness of it.

Later, she let him turn the light on in the corner of the room, and he returned to the bed to study her body with delight, tracing the soft contours with expert hands.

Jane was so relaxed that she could have slept easily, a drugged, peaceful, unknowing sleep. But soon, under the guidance of his skilled touch, she found her desire growing again, disbelieving it at first, thinking that the experience was never to be hers again, having given up hopes for it since the earliest days of marriage.

Barton said nothing. Nor were any words necessary. Slowly his efforts roused her until her body tingled all over. Nor was Jane idle, to his obvious pleasure.

Within a few minutes, they had climbed the same hill again, only this time, knowing the path, they had come more slowly, more surely to the top.

Jane shuddered, uttering a little cry of triumph, and Joe chuckled.

"Surprised *me* too, honey."

He fixed them a drink while Jane put on a nightgown. She couldn't remember when she had felt more rested, more womanly, more satisfied.

"You know, sometimes a person doesn't really know himself," she said, almost to herself. "You just never know what you're capable of, under the right conditions."

Joe grinned at her, then flopped on the bed. "We'd better get to sleep. I've got a rough day tomorrow."

She felt a twinge of disappointment. She wanted to continue, conversationally, the closeness of the past moments, but Joe Barton obviously had no such desire. And why should he, she asked herself? Why should he?

"Okay." She stood, hesitated.

"Sleep with me."

"All right."

She joined him in the bed. Joe went to sleep almost immediately, but Jane lay awake for several moments. She thought of what she had done, thought of Dan for the first time that evening.

Maybe I've needed this, Dan, she thought. Maybe this has purged me, maybe now I can make that extra effort that our marriage needs. Maybe we can start all over again, right from the beginning, and where it was so good back then, it can be that good again.

I *know* it can.

I've never felt better, Dan. You have no idea how really good I feel. Nerveless. Complete. Satisfied as I've never been before in my life.

But you could do that for me too, Dan. If you would.

She smiled gently in the dark room, pleased with her body, pleased with Joe's expertness and with the new resolve she felt toward her personal problems.

She had known the trip to New York would do her good. But she hadn't realized how good it would be.

She drifted off to sleep then, awakening once when the dawn was just breaking to find Joe tugging urgently at her rumpled gown, helping him while still half-asleep, accepting his love eagerly in her drowsiness.

Later, she dropped immediately into an even deeper rest.

CHAPTER NINE

STILL half-drugged from the many pleasures of the night, Jane awoke slowly. She sensed immediately that it was late, and that Joe was gone. Picking up the phone, she learned it was after ten o'clock.

Lazily, she eased out of the mussed bed, stepping out of her gown as she walked to the shower, enjoying the pelting, stinging droplets on her firm flesh.

As she dressed, she found the note Barton had left for her beside her purse.

"I'll be back at four, Sleepy," it said. "Have fun, but be ready to go when I get back. Plane leaves at six. Joe."

She smiled at the prospect of more time in New York, and was really thankful that she hadn't had to accompany him anywhere. The night before now seemed like a wonderful, satisfying dream, but one reality remained. Her resolve to start again with Dan was stronger than ever, and she acted upon it as soon as she had finished breakfast in the hotel coffee shop.

Outside, the day was humid, hot. She walked swiftly toward Fifth Avenue, then more slowly as she searched for the right shop, finally finding it and entering its rich splendor almost timidly.

A salesgirl approached across the heavily carpeted floor, listening to Jane's request, returning swiftly with several diaphanous nightgowns. Jane looked them over carefully. When the right time came with Dan—the time to begin again—she was determined to be properly dressed. She finally selected one, paying almost twenty-five dollars because the price wasn't important, not then, only the results that it would bring.

Outside again, the prized nightgown in a box under her arm, she strolled around the city until three o'clock, returning then to the hotel, packing both her bag and Barton's, so that when he came dashing in at four, everything was ready.

Jane felt a sense of relief that there wasn't time for Joe to make any demands upon her. Not that it hadn't been pleasant. But it was the past now, a past she wanted to gratefully forget so that all her concentration could be on the future.

In the plane, winging through the dusky sky, the fears began. What if Dan had preceded her home, what if Stillwell or Marilyn, innocently or not, mentioned to him about Harry's presence the other night? She knew what he would immediately assume, knew what his reaction would be, especially if he had time alone to think about it, blow it up in his mind before he asked her about it.

By the time the plane arrived, Jane was almost positive that all she dreaded had actually happened. She shared a cab with Joe to her house, silently afraid all the way until the familiar shape of the place loomed out of the darkness, and she saw there were no lights on, no car in the driveway—no Dan, apparently.

"Thanks, Joe," she said as the cab eased to a stop. "I—well, I had a good time."

"Me too, honey. You look kinda done in. Why don't you take tomorrow off, rest up, come back to work Thursday?"

"Oh, I'd love to. But there'll be so much to catch up on," letting her voice trail off, hoping he would convince her that it would be all right for her to spend the day at home.

He did. "One day won't make any difference. And you've earned a day to yourself. There won't be anything for one day that I can't handle. So stay home. That's an order."

"All right," she said gratefully. "Thanks. Again."

The cab driver carried her bag to the front door. Jane inserted her key in the glare of the headlights, stepped inside the welcome darkness of the house as the cab backed out of the driveway and swung toward Barton's address.

Home, she thought. How glad I am to be back.

Her plans to begin again with her husband were so firmly in her mind, it was easy to imagine that they had, in effect, really started, and a great sense of happiness flooded her.

She fixed herself a drink in the kitchen, carried it to the bedroom where she unpacked. Pulling down the blinds, she undressed then donned her new nightgown for the first time, studying herself critically in the full-length mirror behind her closet door.

Her breasts pushed against the thin material, making twin tents of it. Lower, the gown clung to the gentle swell of her stomach, then arched out over her rounded hips. She walked toward the mirror, and the gown clung to her body, outlining her full thighs. It was a gown designed to do a job, and Jane knew she had selected wisely.

Abruptly, she shrugged it off, packing it away carefully in her dresser. This wasn't the time to be caught wearing it. It had to be saved for the special moment, the special attempt they would make, together, soon.

She put on an old pair of lounging pajamas, replaced everything from her suitcase, then went back downstairs to turn out the lights. As she flicked the kitchen switch, she noticed a light at the Andersons and watched, curiously. She saw Harry wander by the window several times then, with relief, she saw Alice.

Well, that took care of that. She didn't think Harry would be bothering her soon again, but Alice being home made it a certainty. Jane went to bed soon afterward, lying awake for a long time as she thought about her trip. She wondered if Joe Barton would be the same boss he had always been, or if he'd expect to savor her body at regular intervals now, now that the trip was behind them.

Please don't, Joe, she thought. It's past, it's all over. We've had our fun. Now let's forget it, like adults.

She was glad she had a day before returning to the station. A day to get used to the idea of their new familiarity, a day to accept it, live with it.

It was raining the next morning, a light, steady drizzle that presaged a full day of dampness. As Jane poured her second cup of morning coffee, the phone rang and she ran to answer it, thinking it was Dan and wanting to know when he would come home, when the new start could begin. But it was Marilyn.

"How was your trip?"

"Fine. Very busy but I got a chance to see a lot of New York."

"I thought I'd come over for awhile—if you're not busy."

"I'm not. Come on." Wishing she could make some excuse but knowing there was none.

She poured a cup for Marilyn, then held the door open for her as she came running across the backyards and into the kitchen. Marilyn was wearing a housedress, low-cut, and her full breasts bobbed gently as she ran, obviously unrestricted by any bra. It was easy for Jane to understand the magnetism such well-displayed charms had for men, why a mailman might change his route after a few exposures to it.

"Wet," Marilyn said.

"You should have worn a coat."

"Too much trouble. Well, Janie, tell me all about it. What did you do, and what did you see. I want to know *every*thing."

"Okay." Jane launched into an expurgated recital of the trip, stressing heavily the way she accompanied Barton on his rounds of the network and agency offices, how she had helped by having at her fingertips information for which he searched. Occasionally, she told Marilyn, Barton would make calls where she wasn't needed, and during those lulls she manager to do her sightseeing. As she related the story to Marilyn, she found it told easily, and knew Dan's version would be familiar.

"What's happened here since I've been gone?" she asked upon conclusion, wanting to know if Dan had been home or tried to reach her, but unwillingly to come right out and ask.

"Nothing. You know how it is around here. Dull dull dull. What did you do all day Sunday by the way?" Her eyes showed her gleaming interest. "I was thinking of having you come over for lunch, but no one answered when I called."

"Oh, I was home, I'll have to admit. But I was so busy getting ready for the trip, and fighting a headache, I just didn't answer the phone all day." The truth sounded funny, and Jane realized it.

"Oh. I thought maybe you'd gone out to the beach again." Her voice was innocent, but the implication was obvious. Jane decided to play it her way.

"But how could I do *that*, Marilyn? I didn't have a car."

"Oh, that's *right*. I guess I thought maybe Harry took you."

"Oh, we wouldn't have gone, not without *you*, Marilyn."

Jane returned Marilyn's bitchy grin, realizing that Marilyn was getting angry at being played with, not wanting to antagonize her, yet not willing to buckle under to her jealous suspicions.

"Oh, I just didn't *know*, after catching—ha—I mean, *seeing* Harry here at your house Saturday night. I mean, we thought maybe you were making *plans*."

"You *did*? Why, we were really talking about *you*, and what we all did at the lake, and everything. But we stopped when you came in, because we knew you didn't want Still to know about it. Did you?"

Marilyn took a deep breath, then dropped her sunny mien, apparently deciding it wasn't worth the effort.

"Well, Jane, you will admit it looked suspicious."

"Really? Harry just came over to borrow some sugar."

"I'll bet."

"Whatever do you mean?" Jane still kept up her heavily-stressed innocence, determined to outdo the girl at her own game.

"Oh, come on, Jane. You and I both know Harry better than that. The only sugar he wanted from you wasn't the kind you put in coffee. Not *my* coffee anyway," and giggled.

"Marilyn, we *do* know what Harry's like. But he's not like that with everyone. There are some people that he just can't get to first base with, and when he realizes it, why he's just like anyone else. As soon as you show him that you're not—ah, available, he'll leave you alone, just like he does me." Her thoughts jumped back to Saturday night and she complimented herself on being a colossal liar.

"Why, he doesn't ever bother me, Janie."

"Isn't that nice? That makes two of us."

Marilyn's face fell as she saw that her cattiness wasn't going to work. "I guess you're right, Jane." She took a deep breath. "Reckon I'll go on home."

"Okay. But don't unless you want to. I think we understand each other, Marilyn."

Their eyes met steadily, unwaveringly, for a moment, then Marilyn nodded coldly and left.

A nervousness came over Jane after the girl had gone. Would it end there? Or was Marilyn mad because Jane had taken the play away from her at the lake? Mad enough to tell Dan? Or even hint about it? Hints would be enough for him, and they didn't have to be subtle either. Dan had always been suspicious. All he needed was a tiny ounce of circumstantial evidence, and she knew what his reaction would be.

The afternoon passed rapidly as Jane prepared for Dan's arrival that evening. Although she hadn't heard from him, no call, no letter, she remembered him saying he'd return in the middle of the week, and to Dan, that was Wednesday.

She mixed a container full of martinis, put it in the refrigerator, then worked diligently at dinner, preparing his favorite foods; steak, creamed cauliflower with white sauce extracted from its cooking juices, baked potato rubbed in olive oil, tossed salad, apple pie.

The final preparations had just been completed when he came in, unannounced, showing neither pleasure nor surprise at seeing her.

"How was your trip?" she asked, taking his raincoat and hanging it up for him.

"All right, I guess."

"How about a martini?"

Dan regarded her suspiciously. "All right."

She joined him in the living room, bringing her own drink, sitting opposite him. "Aren't you going to ask me about *my* trip?"

"You went, huh?"

"Yes. I thought that was understood."

He glared at her. "I told you not to go."

"Dan, we went through that before. Now it's over, I went, I had a good time. I've got travelling out of my system for a long time." She moved her legs deliberately so that her skirt rode well above her knees, hoping to distract him. "I want to tell you all the things I saw, if you'll let me."

"Where were you Sunday?"

"I was here."

"Why didn't you answer the phone?"

"Oh. I wasn't feeling very good. I didn't answer it all day."

"Nuts!"

"Dan!"

"I've heard some phony stories, but that's the topper." He got up swiftly.

"Where are you going?"

"Get some stuff out of the car."

"Dinner'll be ready soon."

"I'm not very hungry."

"I've got all your favorite stuff."

"Why?" he said, whirling on her angrily. "Feeling guilty about something? Tryin' to ease the ol' conscience?"

"Dammit, I—" she paused, controlling her anger. Perhaps she should feel guilt, but she didn't. Her efforts had been directed toward their new start, and now he was spoiling it. "No," she said calmly. "I knew you'd be tired from your trip, and I thought you'd enjoy having a special dinner." Without another word, she returned to the kitchen and continued with her work. She heard him come in and clump around in their bedroom, heard him unpacking, bathing, and knew that she had no reason to resent his suspicions. For once, he was right, and she couldn't admit it.

When dinner was ready and on the table, she called him. He ate his food wordlessly, filling the hungry void of his stomach before tilting back in his chair, studying her as he lit a cigarette.

"When'd you leave?"

"Monday morning."

"What time?"

"Seven fifty."

"Get back?"

"Last night. At seven twenty-six," she added quickly, anticipating his next question.

"Where'd you stay?"

Jane named the hotel, named the room number. When he wanted to know whom she had called upon, she listed the agencies readily, knowing he wouldn't realize if it were the truth or not.

"What'd you do at night?"

"Stayed in my room and watched television," she said, knowing she could never tell him about the nightclubs, not now.

"That's plausible," he said, grinning.

"Well, it's the truth, Dan."

"Sure it is."

Jane felt completely deflated, defeated. Everything was going to be so different, only it wasn't different at all. He was just the same. Somehow, she had to get through to him, had to crack the indifference of a marriage, had to find a way back to the beginning.

It had all seemed so simple in New York. Her intent had been so strong it was just as though the accomplishment would naturally follow. She saw now that it wasn't to be like that, if it was to be at all. It would take something else, and she didn't know what it was.

Dan drank while she did the dishes, drank while they watched TV. At ten, he told her they would go to bed.

"Right now?"

"Right now."

"It's early, Dan."

"I want you—now." He stood before her, weaving slightly.

"Later, Dan, please. Let the drinks wear off a little."

"You don't want me?" he asked slyly.

"It's not that. I want you very much, but I want you sober. Is that too much to ask?"

"You sure you're not just all loved out?"

"That's a mean thing to say." And almost the truth, she thought, almost the truth.

"C'mon, baby."

"You go ahead. I'll bring you a nightcap."

"Okay. Okay." He went to the doorway, grinning. "Don't be long."

"I won't."

In the kitchen, she poured a triple shot over some ice, added a small amount of water, and prayed it would be enough to make him forget sex. He was always hasty when he'd been drinking. And that wasn't right for the beginning-again.

She waited until he called for her angrily to hurry, then took the drink into him. Dan was in bed, the covers pulled up to his naked waist. He took the drink, patted the bed beside him.

"Hop in."

"I want to take a bath."

"Later."

"Please."

"All right," he said, his voice surly.

Jane went into the bathroom and locked the door, running her bath slowly, then slipping into it with pleasure, taking her time. Dan called her twice, and both times she told him she would be right out. Finally, he stopped calling her, and she stepped out of the tub, drying herself slowly.

She donned her pajamas and padded into the bedroom. A snore greeted her. Dan had passed out. He lay in a drunken sleep, his mouth open, snoring.

CHAPTER TEN

J ANE arrived at work the next morning earlier than usual, anxious to see how much work had piled up while she was gone, anxious too to find out how Joe would be, now that they were back home from New York.

She was one of the first to arrive, with the exception of the production crew, who came on at six o'clock, turning on equipment preparatory to the station's seven o'clock sign-on.

The mail was stacked high on her desk, although she could tell that Joe had leafed through it and extracted whatever looked important or interesting to him. Jane began her work immediately, slitting the envelopes, extracting their contents and attaching everything together with a paper clip, making a neat stack for Barton.

As nine o'clock neared, Ruth entered busily, sat down on the edge of Jane's desk, wriggling her fanny until she was comfortable.

"Well?" she said eagerly, her eyes alight.

"Well what?" Jane laughed.

"Tell me about the trip, girl. I want to know all the lurid details."

"I just can't," Jane said, hiding her face with comic shyness.

"Was the trip *that* good?" Ruth fell in with her spirit readily, pretending shocked amazement.

"Better."

"Seriously now, Jane. I really want to hear about it. And quick, before he comes in and you have to edit."

Briefly, Jane related the story of her trip, the same story she had told Dan, except that she admitted the nightclubs to Ruth who wouldn't have believed anything else, knowing Barton and the station expense-account as she did. When Jane was through, Ruth got up to go, then hesitated.

"That was *all?*"

"What else?"

"No pinchy-feely-patty?"

"Oh, the usual amount. But I get that here."

"Listen." Ruth came closer, leaning over the desk, her head close to Jane's. "Did he—did he try anything else?"

"Well, if he did, it was so subtle that I wasn't aware of it," Jane said.

"I'll be damned!"

"Why?"

"I just would've bet ol' Joe would chase you naked through Times Square if he had half a chance. Maybe I've been figuring him wrong."

"Maybe he didn't have half a chance," Jane offered.

"Maybe he talks a better fight than anything."

Jane shrugged. "Anyway I'm glad. It would have been embarrassing if it'd been different."

"Yeah. Well, see you for coffee, girl."

Ruth left and Jane breathed a sigh of relief, hoping that her story had been valid, believable. But why wasn't it? Why did her going to New York with Joe have to mean anything more than it represented? The fact that it *did* wasn't important. Couldn't a man and a woman go on a business trip together, and have it be just a business trip?

The answer to her question was obvious, she knew.

He came into the office then, ending her introspection.

"Rested?" he asked in greeting.

"Definitely. Rarin' to go."

"Good. Quite a bit piled up while we were gone. Let's start out with some dictation. I want to get some stuff out in the noon mail."

Jane picked up her notebook and followed him into his office, feeling a certain concern since she didn't yet know how he would be. Would he expect their new intimacy to be continued? Would he make demands upon her that she wouldn't meet?

But she needn't have worried. Joe started immediately on a pile of letters that demanded answers, dictating steadily until ten o'clock.

"That'll be enough for now," he told her, starting to leave. "I'll be at the Production Meeting if you need me for anything. Get as many of those out by noon as you can."

"Okay."

He paused, smiled for the first time, and patted her gently. "Wotta girl," he said, then left quickly.

Jane returned to her desk with relief. He was the same as he'd ever been. Better really, because he hadn't, apparently, had the touching-feeling-pinching obsession that usually greeted her. Perhaps the trip, as completely satisfying as it had been, had cured whatever it was that needed expression in his hands. She hoped so, hoped that what had happened between them would be a closed book, a nice dream that one remembers but never tries to dream again.

She had finished one letter when Ruth and Phyllis came by to go for coffee, but Jane begged off.

"One of the penalties of time-off," she said. "More work than I can handle."

"Surely he'll let you go for coffee."

"Really, kids, I have to get some letters out by noon. I'll make it up tomorrow."

They had only been gone a few minutes when Charlie Small stuck his head in the door.

"Well well, look who's here."

"Hi, Charlie."

"How was the trip?"

"Fine. Had a wonderful time."

"How 'bout having lunch with me?"

"Thanks, Charlie, but I don't really think I should." No more involvements, she told herself, everything aboveboard, all my concentration on Dan.

"Why?"

"The same ol' bit. I'm a married woman."

"Look, Janie, if you can go to New York with Barton, you can have lunch with me without hurting your reputation. Please. It's important."

Jane thought for a moment, watching the boy, feeling sorry for him, then deciding he was right. There was no harm in it, none at all. "All right, Charlie. Twelve o'clock?"

"Fine." His face lit in a handsome grin. "We'll have a ball."

"No ball. Just lunch."

"Oh sure! That's what I meant. Thanks, Janie."

"I'll see you at twelve."

She wondered what it was that he considered important, then forgot about it in the press of her work. Barton came back later, leaning over her shoulder, his hand sneaking under her arm and resting against the side of her breast. Jane plucked the hand away gently, and he laughed, going into his office.

Charlie came by for her right after his weather show, and they walked two blocks to a restaurant of his choice.

"Someplace different," he told her. "I get tired of that same old place everyday."

They ordered sandwiches and iced tea. Jane waited for him to begin the conversation, but their lunch came and he still hadn't said anything, other than to comment on how nice she looked and how he had missed her while she was gone. They finished the sandwiches, ordered and ate pie, and the waiter brought the check; Jane could wait no longer.

"Charlie?"

"Yeah, honey?"

"You said there was something important you wanted to talk about?"

"Yeah. But—well, this isn't the place, Jane."

"Oh?"

"But it is important. More important than you can imagine. Look, I know what," he said brightly, as though the idea had just struck him. "When you get through work, come by my place for a few minutes. We—ah—we can have privacy there, and I can talk to you."

He was obviously nervous, and Jane found him at once transparent, amusing—and pathetic.

"I can't do it, Charlie," she told him gently.

"*Please.*"

"I can't. For one thing, I have to go right home and fix supper. For one thing," she repeated. "There are other reasons and you know what they are."

"But this is im*por*tant."

"So is fixing supper for my husband."

"Janie!" he said, and his face was anguished. "I can't tell you what it is, but it *is* very important, you've got to believe me."

Jane felt herself flattered by his attention, his desire to see her alone, and she asked herself if there would be any harm in going to see him for a few minutes. She could always tell Dan that Barton kept her late, catching up from the trip. And her curiosity was piqued by his repetition of the importance of this mysterious something.

"Don't you trust me, Janie?"

"Of course I do, Charlie."

"Gosh, you don't have to be afraid of me."

"I'm not."

"Then—will you come?"

"If you're sure it'll just be a few minutes."

"It will," he said hastily, happily, unable to really believe she would come.

"Because that's all I can stay. And it's not a social call, you understand that?"

"Yes."

Jane knew she shouldn't have agreed, and told herself she was doing the wrong thing after they returned to the station and the afternoon's work. But there's really no harm in him, she argued silently. He's just a kid and he has a crush on me—and, dammit, I like it. If he has some problem I can help him with, and it just takes a few minutes, and no one's the wiser, then why shouldn't I do it?

So thinking, she accepted what she would do, and put it out of her mind.

The afternoon passed quickly. Joe Barton was in and out of his office, two film salesmen came to see him, taking him away for the better part of an hour while they showed him the pilot film of a new syndicated show their company was producing. Jane's work load gradually eased as she directed her efforts toward it, and when the afternoon coffee break came, she took fifteen minutes and went with the girls, answering their questions about the trip. They all professed their envy of her good fortune, and Jane chuckled to herself as she thought of the expressions that would cross their faces if she told them the whole truth about the trip, and about the night with Joe.

But she said nothing, other than to exclaim over the rich appointments of some of the agency and network offices, and tell the same tale of busy hours, some sightseeing, one nightclub.

She saw that they were satisfied with her recital and was glad. In a few days the trip would be largely forgotten, everything would be back to normal, and she could drop her guard a little bit.

After work, she walked to Charlie's apartment, feeling a quivering of excitement in the act, repressing it by repeating that it was important and harmless. He lived in a brick apartment building four blocks from the station. There was no one in the lobby. Jane walked up to the third floor, not wanting to use the elevator, fearful that someone else from KLKS might live there, not wanting to run into anyone unexpectedly who would wonder or ask what she was doing there.

She knocked lightly on Charlie's door, and he opened it immediately, as though he had been waiting, watching for her.

"Come in."

Jane stepped inside the apartment as Charlie closed and locked the door. She saw it was a typical lodging place for a young bachelor. It hadn't been dusted for days. The rooms were small, and she could see dirty dishes in the sink, an unmade bed beyond in the tiny bedroom

"How about a drink?"

"What have you got?"

"Beer is all," he said hopefully.

"Beer sounds good."

"I'll fix it."

Jane glanced around the living room while she waited. There was a picture of a middle-aged woman on a small table, and she knew from the resemblance that it was his mother. On one wall, a calender hung, the girl standing with legs apart, hands on hips, wearing only briefs as she thrust her huge, naked breasts into the picture. There were two ashtrays, one from a hotel in Miami, another with a nude girl's figure curved around its edge. There was a place between her legs to put out cigarettes. Several magazines lay on the coffee table.

She heard him pouring the second glass and directed her attention back to the doorway through which he came with the beer.

"Here's how," he said, and they both drank the cold liquid thirstily. "Boy that hits the spot."

"Very good."

"You want to hear some records, Janie?" He sat beside her on the couch, smiling happily. "I didn't have time to really fix the place up, like I wanted to. It's kind of a mess, isn't it?"

"I hadn't noticed," she lied.

"How about some music?" he repeated eagerly. "I've got some new Christy."

"Charlie, I really can't stay long. Don't you think you should tell me what it is you have on your mind?" She said it gently, but tried to impart her haste.

"Well—"

"Now Charlie, I came, didn't I?" she said, sensing that he was hurt—or pretending to be—that she couldn't stay longer.

"It's not easy to say," he told her mysteriously. "Tell me about your trip first."

"Charlie. I can't stay long. The trip isn't important, not right now."

"Did Barton give you any trouble?"

"No."

"Are you sure?"

"Of course," she said, surprised at his persistence.

"I don't believe it."

"Why?"

"Because Barton's not like that. I think he took you to New York because he wanted to try to make you. Janie, I hate that bastard!" he said vehemently.

"Well, Charlie, if it helps any, I'm telling you the truth. He was very well behaved, all the time."

The boy leaned closer to her. "He didn't try anything?"

"That's what I said."

"I *know* he did."

"Now listen, Charlie. I'm telling you he didn't. But it's not any of your business, one way or the other. So if you have something important to tell me, do it, or else I'll have to leave, right now."

"Don't." He put his hand on her knee as though to keep her from moving.

"Then let's forget the trip for awhile," she chided him.

"All right." He set his beer glass down on the table, but his hand remained on her knee, lightly, unmoving. "I—I've been thinking a lot about you the last few days. I always have. I mean, thought about you, ever since I've known you." His hand moved up her leg an inch, but he kept his eyes on the ceiling as he talked. "I've always liked you. You know, we've kidded around a lot, you 'n me, at the station, about going out together and everything, well, you know what I mean."

His hand moved higher, almost to the top of her stocking, and she felt it begin to tremble. She took his hand in hers and moved it away.

"That's enough, Charlie."

"I love you," he said urgently, turning to her, throwing his arms around her awkwardly. His mouth was on hers before she knew what was happening, his lips kissing her. Startled, it was a moment before she pushed him away.

"Don't, Charlie."

"But I love you. Didn't you hear me say it? I love you, and I need you, honey. Let me love you, please, please let me." The words tumbled out of his mouth as though from a bursting dam, as though he had rehearsed what he wanted to say and now was afraid he wouldn't get all the words in. "I've loved you right from the start, right from the first day I ever saw you at the station. I know you're married, I know all about that, but I love you too, more than your husband ever could, and I want you. You're so pretty, you drive me crazy, please, Janie. I'm begging." As he talked he put his arm around her again, trying to kiss her as he finished. When she moved her head, his lips went to her throat, the bare skin above her square-cut blouse. Touched, Jane didn't resist. She patted his head lightly, feeling a sympathy for him.

She knew she would have to discourage him, refuse his love, and didn't want to hurt him.

Charlie accepted her lack of resistance as acceptance, and his hand closed on her breast, mashing it too hard in his exhuberance, hurting her.

"Ouch," she said, removing his hand.

"I'm sorry." His eyes were pained as they found hers. "I didn't mean to hurt you."

"I know. It's all right." She smiled at him tenderly. "You've got to stop, Charlie."

He moved to kiss her mouth, and she let him, opening her lips to his kiss, curious about it, accepting his darting tongue briefly. Charlie moaned, pushing her skirt up, trying to force her back on the couch.

"No," she said sharply.

"You *got* to."

"No, I said, Charlie. Let me up." His hands were all over her, searching her body roughly, rudely. He was like a young puppy in his enthusiasm, but she finally forced him to sit up while she straightened her clothes. "Don't ever do that, Charlie," she told him, torn between a desire to experiment and anger at his roughness.

"Please go to bed with me, Janie."

"Charlie!"

"Well, how are you *supposed* to ask a girl?"

Jane hesitated, then laughed. "I don't know. I don't think you ask at all. It's just something that happens when both people want it to."

"Well, I want it to happen. Don't you?"

"Charlie—you're a nice boy. I like you, really I do. But I'm married. You keep forgetting that, and it makes a difference—a big difference."

"But you went to New York with Barton."

"That was business."

"Don't give me that, Janie. He took you so he could—go to bed with you."

"You're wrong."

"Why won't you love *me?*"

Jane stood up, looking down at his desperate pleading face. "Is this what was so important?"

"That I love you? Yes."

"No, Charlie, I don't mean that. I mean this wanting me to go to bed with you."

"It's important. To me. I guess I'm the only one, though," he added miserably.

Jane didn't know what to say. She liked Charlie, didn't want to hurt him. Yet she didn't feel that she could do what he asked. It would jeopardize everything, and she was determined not to do that. She wished she hadn't come, but she had, and now she had to leave as gracefully as possible. She started to say something to him and realized his eyes were filled with tears.

"Charlie?"

"Don't laugh at me. I can't help it."

"Don't cry, honey. It's not the end of the world." She hugged him with a sisterly affection. "Honest."

"Can I tell you something?"

"Sure."

"I'm a virgin."

"Well, honey, we all are for awhile."

"But guys nineteen aren't. Not many of 'em anyway. And I'm scared, Jane, scared when I get a chance to—to go to bed with a girl I won't know what to do. Or be able to do it. I've got to find *out.*" He sobbed as he put his head on her shoulder, and she felt a wave of pity sweep over for him. If things were different, she thought, I could help him. Even last week, I might have reacted in another way. But not now.

"You'll find out, Charlie. Pretty soon."

"With you?"

"Not with me."

"Who then? Do you know anyone who goes around doing favors for nineteen-year-old jerks?"

"No. But, sooner or later, Charlie, you'll find the right girl—someone your own age."

"Girls my own age are silly."

"Not the right one."

"They don't know any more about sex than I do," he protested, bitterly. "They get scared before you even get started good."

"Maybe they're scared because they don't want anything to happen before they're married. And did you ever think it might be fun, sort of experimenting with a girl who didn't know all about it, finding the secrets and pleasures for yourselves?" she asked, hoping by her words to soften whatever disappointment he might feel.

"They just don't appeal to me, Janie. Not like you do."

"Charlie, I'm flattered that I appeal to you. But there's no future for us. Not with me married, and quite happily."

"But I love you," repeating the words as though they contained a magic that would open all doors, solve all problems, cure all ills.

"I know you do. And I appreciate it."

"But you don't love me?"

"I'm fond of you."

"You could learn to love me."

"No. It's different, Charlie. Fondness and love are worlds apart sometimes."

"But why?"

"I don't know what to say, baby. If I knew the words that would make you feel better, I'd say them. If I loved you, I'd tell you. But I want us to stay friends. Please understand, Charlie. Friends."

"That's all?"

"That's all."

Charlie took a deep breath and stepped away from her, his eyes hurt, his mouth quivering. "Want another beer before you go?"

Jane shook her head, then smiled. "Thanks, Charlie. Thanks for understanding and being a gentleman."

"It's not easy."

"I know it's not. And I appreciate it."

"Thanks for coming by," he said at the door, and she found his lack of enthusiasm humorous and touching.

"I enjoyed it, Friend," she said, and extended her hand. Charlie took it, shook hands with her shortly. "Bye," she told him, and walked down the hall, down the stairs. She felt sorry for him, but proud of herself as she reentered the busy streets and ran to catch her bus.

CHAPTER ELEVEN

HER pride in her behavior with Charlie grew as she rode the bus home.

It wasn't as though the boy wasn't tempting, she thought. He has a good build, nice features, and his burden of virginity was somewhat appealing. No, it wasn't as though it was easy, turning him down, resisting the temptation to experiment.

But I did it. And for one reason. The beginning-again.

As the bus slowed, approaching her stop, she walked to the rear door, then hastened to her house, wishing it wasn't so late. The neat rows of ranch-style houses stretched evenly ahead of her, and she felt a glow of pleasure in their symmetry, the lawns manicured, trees growing again in the yards where a hasty developer had leveled all growth not too long before, claiming it was necessary in order to mass-produce at a reasonable price.

Dusk was descending over the neighborhood as she arrived home, seeing Dan's car parked in the driveway and feeling relieved. She recognized an existing—but until then unacknowledged fear that he might have taken umbrage at her lateness, and gone off angrily.

Jane opened the door, noticed there were no lights on in the house.

"Dan?"

There was no answer. She lit a lamp in the living room, checked the kitchen, bedrooms. Nothing. Nobody.

"Dan?"

He wasn't in the house, nor was he in the backyard. She looked up and down the rear areas, but saw so activity that might have attracted him.

He'll be back in a minute, she told herself. Maybe he just walked down to the store for something, knowing even as she thought it that he never walked to the store, always drove or had her go.

Jane started dinner, expecting to hear him any moment. When it was time to either go ahead and complete the dinner, or hold it in abeyance, she decided with a trace of annoyance to wait. She mixed herself a collins, paced with it nervously, wondering why he hadn't left her a note. Then she wondered if perhaps something had happened to him, some accident.

After another half-hour, she decided to search for him actively, and crossed to Marilyn's house, hoping she might have seen him leave, that he might have mentioned something to her. She let herself in the kitchen door, availing herself of the communal privilege they had all established, walked through the dark kitchen.

"Anybody home?" she called, entering the living room, then stopping, shocked at what she saw.

"Hi," Marilyn said unsteadily. Her blouse was unbuttoned, hanging open, exposing her bosom. Her hair was mussed, lipstick awry. Dan sat on the couch, a drink in his hand, grinning drunkenly at her.

"Surprise," Jane said dryly.

"Yeah," Marilyn said, and giggled as she tried to button her blouse with one fumbling hand, spilling some of her drink on the carpet as she concentrated unsuccessfully on the buttons.

"Where were you?" Dan asked.

"Does that matter?"

"Sure it matters," he announced, his voice surly. He got to his feet after a momentary struggle for balance. "You're late. I'm glad

Marilyn here was home so a guy could have a li'l comp' ny while he waited."

"Oh sure. Are you ready to come home?"

"No."

"Where's Stillwell, Marilyn?"

"He's—ah—at a—scout meeting, Janie. Wanna drink?"

"I don't think so."

"Go ahead," Dan said. "Do you good."

"I'll be home whenever you feel like coming," she told him cooly and started to leave.

"Wait!" he said.

"What?"

"Siddown a minute."

"And be entertained by your half-naked slut! No thanks."

"Shut up!"

"You've got me all wrong," Marilyn protested, pouting.

"I wanna ask you somethin'," Dan said, staggering close to her. "I wanna ask you somethin' an' I want you to tell me the truth."

"Well, ask then, because I'm not staying long."

"Aw right. What was Harry doin' at our house las' Saturday night?"

Jane noticed that Marilyn was grinning slyly, and knew the girl had told Dan. There was no other way he could've found out. "He came over to borrow some sugar."

"I'll jus' *bet* he did."

Marilyn snickered, turning her face hurriedly when her eyes met Jane's.

"Well?" Dan went on. "Did he get any?"

"Of course."

Her husband paused, wondering if she meant her answer as he had meant his question, then became confused and angry. "Is that what you do when my back's turned, when I leave town on a business trip, have guys like Harry in to paw you, you bitch?"

He tried to slap her, but she ducked his blow easily. His face reddened. He snorted, then turned to Marilyn who was watching with an expression that was half-pleased, half-afraid. "Gimme another drink."

"Okay," the girl said, with a glance at Jane.

"You'd better come home before Still gets here," she told Dan, without any real anger, knowing she had no right to judge.

"I'll come home when I get good and damn ready."

"All right." Jane turned abruptly and left, fighting the hurt, the tears that wanted to come. She slammed the Anderson's kitchen door and ran home, turned off the simmering dinner and went into the bedroom, locking the door and throwing herself down on the bed, dry-eyed.

What sort of a mess is this life of mine coming to? she asked herself. Is this my punishment for Harry, for Joe?

She couldn't blame Marilyn, not really. She knew that telling Dan about Harry was the girl's way of getting even for the trip to the lake when Jane had taken the play away from her. No, she couldn't blame her. Nor could she blame Dan. If stuff like that was available and kept throwing itself at a man, it would be awfully hard to keep hands off. She just hoped he would take her advice and come home before Marilyn's husband returned from his scout meeting. Stillwell was a mild-mannered guy, but there was a limit to what a man would take.

Tonight was going to be the beginning-again, she thought bitterly. Big deal. That's a project we'd better put in mothballs, store away, forget about.

The tears came then, as she considered the defeat of her plans, her high hopes. She'd wanted to start over again with him so badly. But it took two to tango, and her desire alone wasn't enough and never would be.

She thought of Charlie, and wished she had stayed, wished even that she had helped him with his 'problem'. It would have been no worse if she had, certainly. And he loves me, she thought.

Maybe he's the answer. She imagined what it would be like, living with him. He was so young, there were six big years between them. Only did he mean it, about loving me? she thought. Or perhaps did he think a plea of love would get me in bed with him?

Her mind dwelled on the boy, on his body, and what it would be like, bedding him down in his young virility. It would either be great or lousy. At that age there was seldom any in-between.

It occurred to her that she could easily go back to town, that Dan might not come home for hours. There was no reason that she had to wait there for him, locked in her room, anticipating the drunken, sullen return.

But even as the ease of such a decision struck her, she knew she couldn't, wouldn't do it. There was something to be faced right there, and running off to the arms of Charlie was no way to settle it.

If there was *any* way.

She heard the kitchen door slam shut.

Welcome home, Danny boy, she thought. I hope you made it before Still came home.

She could hear Dan staggering through the kitchen, banging into table and chairs. He reached the living room, and she heard a heavy chair go over. Then there was silence—a long silence.

Jane unlocked the door, opened it quietly and listened. Soon she heard Dan's snoring. She shrugged. "This is getting to be a habit." Jane undressed and got into bed, saying bitterly, "Three cheers for our beginning-again!"

CHAPTER TWELVE

BREAKFAST THE next morning was a grim affair. Dan complained that his waffles were too brown, ignored her one or two mild attempts at starting a conversation and questioned her choice of a dress to wear to work.

"Have you worn that before?"

Jane glanced down at the yellow print dress with its full skirt, square-cut bodice. "Several times."

"I mean to work."

"No. I don't think so."

"Don't you think it's a little suggestive?"

"What do you mean?" she asked, taking offense at his criticism of her selection.

"Well, you just bent over the table and I could see down your front like you didn't have a dress on."

"Dan, I'm certainly more careful at work than I am around home."

"Why wear anything you have to be careful in?" he asked, pressing the point.

"Because I like this dress, and I hadn't given a thought to anything except wanting to look nice, until you brought this whole thing up."

"That's what I mean."

"Well, I'm wearing it, so let's drop the whole subject, if you don't mind too much." Jane fought to keep her anger under control. Sometimes Dan could see evil in the simplest things. She was tempted to bring Marilyn into the conversation, but decided against it. It was almost time to leave for work and she hated to leave home feeling upset, or with an argument between them.

"You gonna be home early tonight?" he asked.

"Regular time I guess. Why?"

"The Anderson's barbeque. You didn't forget it, did you?"

"No. Of course not." But she had. It had slipped her mind completely.

And that was the way it went until she arrived at KLKS. It was a relief to be there. She plunged into her work.

Joe Barton's arrival interrupted her. He stood beside her desk, saying nothing, and Jane knew he was looking down her dress. Her first impulse was to sit back in her chair, but decided that would be school-girlish. If he wanted to look, let him.

"I'm going to clean up a few things," he said, "then I want to talk to you. Privately."

Jane looked up at him, questioningly, but Barton only smiled and went into his office. He didn't delay for very long. In just a few minutes he called for her to come into his office.

"Close the door," he said.

Jane closed it.

"Lock it."

"Lock it?"

Barton nodded, smiling, and Jane did as he directed.

"Now come over here."

She walked close to his desk, pausing in front of it, but he motioned for her to come around by his chair.

"What is it, Mr. Barton?" she asked, although she felt she knew, and wondered what she could do about it.

"Just want to talk to you, Janie. And call me Joe, huh?"

When she stood beside his chair, he put his hand on her stockinged leg in back of her knee.

"We haven't really had a chance to be alone together since we got back from New York."

"No," she admitted in a small voice.

"How's everything going?" His hand moved up her leg a few inches.

"Okay."

"No trouble with your husband?"

"Oh, no." She wished he would remove his hand, but didn't know how to ask it without offending him. Then his hand moved higher up her leg until it rested on the bare flesh above her stocking. Jane felt the desire start, but warned herself. She had to fight it, she had to refuse him what he was going to want, she had to stay true for Dan. That much she had decided, and she knew she had to stick to it if she was ever to accomplish what she wanted of her marriage. She had had her release, her wild fling. Now that was in the past and had to stay there.

"I just learned this morning that I'll be going to Los Angeles next month. For a week."

"Oh?"

"Sound interesting?"

"What—ah, what's the occasion?" It was hard to keep her mind on her words as his hand crept up to her panties, his fingers playing with the edge of them.

"NAB meeting. Combination of business and pleasure really."

"That should be fun for you."

"For us. If you want to go."

Jane cast about for an excuse. "When is it?"

"The eighteenth to the twenty-fifth."

"Oh," trying to sound disappointed. "We've got relatives coming on the twentieth. They'll probably stay two weeks." It would be easy enough later to say they hadn't been able to come, if Joe made a point of it.

Barton was genuinely disappointed. "That's a pity. I was hoping we might make quite a few trips together. The last one was so—successful," grinning at the word as he grasped her buttock and spun her into his lap. His mouth sought hers and she gave him her lips, trying to think of a graceful way to end this. She didn't want to come right out and tell him to stop. It would sound too prudish and it might make him mad. There had to be another way.

The phone on his desk rang, and Jane thought her salvation might be at hand. But Joe indicated she should be quiet, and leaned forward, Jane still firmly in his lap, and picked up the receiver.

"Barton."

He listened a moment. "I'm tied up right now. Will be for another thirty minutes or so. I'll call you back."

Again he listened. "Okay. Thirty minutes or so." Then he hung up the receiver and leaned back in his chair, pulling Jane with him, his hand resting on the dress where a full, jutting breast pushed against it. He sighed contentedly, then pulled her head down to his again. His hand left her breast and rested for a moment on her knee, then gently moved under her dress, past her stockings, higher. Involuntarily, Jane squirmed—pushed his hand away.

"What's the matter?" he asked.

"Nothing," she said weakly, still afraid to come right out and ask him to stop.

Barton assumed she wanted him to go slower, for he returned to fondling her breast through the material of the dress, kissing her lingeringly. Jane felt herself being aroused, but her mind still remained stronger than her emotions and physical feelings.

But how can I stop him? she asked herself. She thought that conversation might help, might take his mind off her body.

"How's everything going?" she asked lightly. Joe looked at her with a puzzled expression, not answering.

When his hands started unbuttoning her dress, Jane decided to try another approach.

"Ouch," she said, forcing a pained expression. "I've got a cramp in my leg." She got off his lap before he could say anything, and limped around the office, rubbing her leg as though rubbing out the pain of a cramp. "Damn!" She threw the word in, hoping it would make her act seem more sincere.

Barton got up and followed her about solicitously. Finally she knew she had played the imaginary cramp for all it was worth.

"Whew," she said, sitting in a single chair, grinning up at him innocently. "That hurt."

"Is it all gone now?"

"Yes."

"Stand up, Janie."

"Joe—"

"Stand up!"

Slowly, she stood. Dam it, if that hadn't taken his mind off his desire, what would?

Barton pulled her against his body. His fingers finished unbuttoning her dress, and he pulled the top part down, exposing her brassiered breasts. He led her to the couch, sitting beside her, his hand reaching over her shoulder and down, inside the cups of her bra.

Why doesn't someone come, she thought? Come and knock on the door. Why isn't there an emergency of some sort, where he *has* to leave?

He pulled her half around, bending her head back with a savage kiss, unfastening her bra as he did so. Jane tried to push him back. He resisted her effort until the bra was loose, then he pulled the cups away. His hands grasped her flesh, his head lowered, kissing.

"Joe?"

"Uh."

"What if someone comes?"

"They won't."

"But—"

"Just pay attention to what we're doing, baby. Don't worry about anything else."

His abrupt answer angered her, but she still retained the slight hope that something would happen. As a last resort she knew she could stop him, *had* to stop him, but she didn't want to do it that way if she could possibly help it.

He left her upper body then, pushing his hands under her dress again, tugging at her undergarments.

"You'll wrinkle my dress."

Joe paused, then sat back. "Take it off then."

Jane stood up, hesitated a moment, as though in that fragment of time something would occur that would make her next words unnecessary. But nothing happened, and she knew she had to face it. She took a deep breath.

"No."

Barton looked at her, at first uncomprehending, then with disbelief.

"What do you mean, 'no'?"

"I—I can't."

"Why?"

He was forcing her to answer. She wanted to stall it out, give herself time to think of a reason he might accept, but she knew there was none. There was nothing to do but face the unpleasantness.

"I—I don't want to."

"Well! That's a switch."

"I'm sorry."

Joe held out his hands, palms upward, indicating his angry confusion. "Is this the same girl who went to New York with me? It was all right then, wasn't it? Seems to me you kinda *liked* it, even."

"I did."

"So?"

"So that was then. This is now, and what's done is done. That doesn't mean it's going to keep on like it was. Joe—"

"You turn it off and on like a faucet?"

"It's not like that. But that trip to New York helped me get a lot of things out of my system. Thanks to you, I did. But it's past. Now I'm trying to make my marriage work again, and if I'm going to do it sincerely, then I've got to be true." Jane took another deep breath, watching for his reaction, seeing the fury gather in his face. "It's as simple as that." Jane retrieved her bra and began putting it on.

"You bitch."

"No, Joe," she protested.

"I can't think of a better word."

"Can't you understand *my* side of it? I enjoyed New York, and you know it. But that was a no-strings-attached deal. Why isn't that fair?"

"Because I want you—now! That's why it's not fair. Hell, Janie, who's to know?"

"Me. I'll know."

"Is this husband of yours worth it?"

"I don't know." She fastened her bra and pulled her dress up to her shoulders. "That's what I'm going to find out. But if I discover that he *is* worth it, then I want to be worthy of him." She turned her back to Barton. "Button me, please."

"I don't like this, Janie. I don't like this at all." He buttoned her rapidly. "You're making a mistake."

"I don't think so, Joe. But—if I am, well, maybe we can talk about that trip again."

Barton shook his head. "Right now—or never."

"Don't put it that way."

"That's the way I feel, baby. Better think it over."

Jane shook her head, not trusting herself to say anything.

Barton shrugged, let his eyes flick over her body one more time, then turned abruptly and left the office, slamming the door shut.

Jane hastened to put on more lipstick and comb her hair before anyone saw her. She hoped Joe would get over being angry.

She could understand how he felt, especially after her willing-ness in New York. It hurt a man to be primed for a woman and then be turned down. But there were two sides to it, and he had to understand her problems too, had to give some thought to what she was trying to do, and why it was important to her to be chaste, until she had had the chance she wanted with Dan.

Joe didn't return to his office before lunch. When the girls came by, Jane pleaded a headache and stayed in her office except for a few minutes when she went upstairs and purchased a candy bar and a soft drink to tide her over.

But Joe Barton didn't return.

When calls came for him, she took the message or the caller's name, telling them he was busy elsewhere in the building and she would have him call at his earliest convenience.

Finally, after three o'clock, he came back. The drinks he had had at lunch were obvious. "Any calls?"

"Yes." Jane handed him the messages. Barton took them without another word and went into his office, closing the door.

Jane felt depressed. Dammit, he shouldn't still be mad at me, she thought. Who does he think he is?

Barton stayed in his office until four-thirty, when he left wordlessly.

"Good night," Jane said, calling the words after him, but he didn't bother to acknowledge hearing her. Slowly, she began put-ting her things away, clearing her desk top for the night.

Well, if that was the way he wanted it to be, then that would be the way he'd get it. She couldn't really believe he could stay angry with her, not after New York. But it was apparently going to take longer than she expected, so that was that.

She had reconciled herself to that when Charlie thrust his head around the corner, saw she was alone, and came in. His face was troubled, serious.

"What's the matter, Charlie-boy?"

"I've got to talk to you."

"Okay," she said, leaning back in her chair. It was only quarter of five.

"Not here."

"Where?"

"My place."

"Now, Charlie, we went through that. Remember?"

"This is different, Janie. It's important. I mean really."

Jane sensed from his manner that he was serious. "When, Charlie?"

"Tonight—when you get off."

She shook her head. "I can't tonight. One of the neighbors is having a barbeque. I've got to get home and be there with my husband."

"This is more important," Charlie said slowly.

"Well, what *is* it?"

"You'll have to wait. We have to be alone."

"Come on, Charlie, it can't be all that bad."

"It is."

"Why be so mysterious?" she asked brightly, hoping she could loosen him up a little. He was watching her with a curious mixture of hatred, love and desire, and it puzzled her.

"It's about your trip."

"To New York?"

He nodded.

"I've told you about that."

"Not the truth."

"Now listen, Charlie—"

"No! *You* listen. I know all about it. And I've got to tell you about it, before you get hurt. But this isn't the place. So you'll come to my apartment." He got up abruptly and stormed out of the office.

For a moment, Jane didn't know what to do. Her first tendency was to ignore him, but the feeling persisted that he knew *something*.

She sighed, realizing she would have to go to Charlie's place to find out. At five, she left the station and walked swiftly to Charlie's apartment. She climbed the stairs, becoming more and more fearful with every step of what she might learn.

Charlie had been waiting for her, and opened the door as she came down the hall, not waiting for her knock.

"Come in." He held a drink in his hand, and looked as though he had taken a fast stiff belt to get started. "What'll you drink? I bought me a bottle today. Got soda and ginger ale to go with it. Li'l fancier than beer, huh?"

"Charlie, I just want to know what you have to tell me, that's all."

"Better have a drink. You'll need it." He laughed lightly, toasted her with his glass, then downed the liquid. "What'll it be?"

"Ginger ale, I guess."

Jane waited impatiently while he fixed her drink, then another for himself. She sipped from the glass he handed her as she sat on the couch, knowing the minutes were ticking by. "Come on, Charlie. What is it?"

"You don't really want me to hurry, do ya?"

"Yes," she said simply.

"You really had me fooled," he said.

"Fooled?"

"Yeah. I was really believin' all you told me about that damn trip. What a sucker, huh?"

"You don't think I told you the truth?"

"I know damned well you didn't!" He proceeded to list for her the room number at the hotel in New York, the time they had arrived, the clothes she wore. "Convinced?"

"I'm convinced that you know where I stayed and what I wore. And that you can read an airplane schedule."

"Okay, honey, you asked for it. Joe made you in New York. And not just once either. You didn't go anyplace with him—'working'—like you said, either. You just went along for the loving."

"Charlie! I don't know where you heard all that, but I can't say I think much of your source."

"Oh?" Charlie laughed. "Well, how about this? You've got a mole that only a lover could discover." He waited, expectantly, smiling as the horrible truth dawned on her. She did indeed have a mole. Joe Barton had seen it while he dallied in the hotel room—with the light on. Joe Barton!

The realization that the truth about her trip to New York was out sickened her, and she sank into a chair, her eyes closed as she fought the nausea that enveloped her.

Her bluffing was no good any longer. She'd kept telling herself that the trip was in the past, that she could forget it and that would be the end of it. Now she knew she'd only been kidding herself.

"How do you know all this?" she asked him, her voice tired and strained.

"So it *is* true, huh?" he asked, gleefully, leaning close to her.

Jane nodded without looking at him.

"And all the time you kept tellin' me nothing happened. An' me, dumb bastard that I am, I *believed* you. I really did. Boy you must've laughed at me, huh? Dumb ol' Charlie, falling for your innocent story, falling in love with you and wanting to believe you."

Jane looked up at him, saw his lip quivering with hurt and anger. "What do you want me to say, Charlie?"

"Nothing. Nothing at all." He got up and went into the tiny kitchen, mixing himself another drink.

"You still haven't answered my question, Charlie."

"Which one?"

"How did you find out?"

"Do you care?"

"Please don't play games with me."

"Okay, okay. This afternoon I was hanging out in the lounge, trying to get a nap in one of the chairs. I guess I was kinda slumped down so no one could see me—and in came Barton and Dawson. Barton was telling Dawson all about the trip and what a hot babe you were and how Dawson oughta try to figure a way he could get out of town for awhile, and take you along to 'work' with him." Charlie paused, and Jane saw that he was almost in tears as he recalled the episode. "Well, he described you," Charlie continued, "so that I know what your body looks like as though I'd studied it all my life. 'Course, Dawson does too. Joe told *all* about it. It made me *sick*."

Jane sat listlessly in the chair. Well, that was that. If Barton had wanted to pay her back for her refusal to cooperate with him that morning, then he had taken a cruel avenue. But pay her back he had—and in spades.

She knew that this wasn't the end of it, either. This kind of thing spread and spread, like wildfire, and there was no telling where it would stop.

Charlie was staring at her, and she smiled at him weakly. "Thanks."

"For what?"

"For telling me. It's good to know where you stand. And who your friends are," she added bitterly. That sonuvabitch Joe! She'd have something to tell him tomorrow, and that was for sure.

Charlie, who had been watching her with what could have been hatred, changed suddenly, and dropped to his knees beside her chair. "I'm sorry."

"That's all right. I guess I even appreciate it, although that's hard to believe."

"I didn't want to tell you—but I knew I had to, honey. You had to know what Barton was saying, even if it hurt—and I know it did."

"Yes."

"Why didn't you tell *me* though? Don't you trust me?" "It would have hurt you too, Charlie. I told you, I'm fond of you. I—well, the New York trip was the end of it, I thought. I had to go away and be wild for awhile. Then I wanted to come back and be myself, and work hard for the things that matter to me. Do you understand?"

Charlie nodded slightly. "I think so."

"I'm not like that, Charlie. Not really. But sometimes you just have all you can take of something, just all you can stand and you have to blow your cork or explode. That's how it was with me. And I'll probably have a long time to regret it."

Charlie came closer and put his head in her lap, his hands gripping her legs. "I could kill that Barton."

"Joe was just getting even with me."

"For what?"

Briefly, she told him of Barton's morning request and her refusal.

"That bastard!" he said, his face filled with pain. Charlie pushed himself up until he was occupying half the chair with her. His hand ran through her hair gently, then caressed her cheek. Jane closed her eyes and submitted to his gentleness. It felt good, and she needed consolation.

They were jammed into the chair, half facing each other, and the position was uncomfortable, but she made no move to get up. She knew he was hurt, and wanted to comfort him. Poor Charlie, she thought. Getting a crush on me, then having me turn him down, then hearing something like *this* from Barton. He must wonder why this ol' world is so cruel.

She moved her face until she could kiss him, pressing her lips against his gently. His pleasure was instantly obvious.

He returned her kiss with added pressure, and his hand rested tentatively on her breast. "I love you, Janie," he whispered.

"No, Charlie. Not after what you heard. You couldn't."

"I do."

"You feel sorry for me. And you want me. But it's not love, honey. Believe me."

"I know love when I feel it. I'm not a little kid, Janie."

He was pleading with her to agree with him, and she did, thinking there would be no harm in it certainly. He needed reassurance and that was the least she could give him.

His hand was still on her breast. He kissed her again, pushing against her. It was apparent that he didn't know how to proceed.

"I love you," he said again.

Jane smiled inwardly. She knew what he was doing, saying the words while he thought up the next move. It reminded her of her high school days, the petting in the back seat. Usually even the boys known as lovers around the school turned out to be fumbling, unsure novices when it came down to cases. There had been exceptions. But not many.

Charlie's hand moved down her side, reaching the edge of her dress, resting on her stockinged knee. She felt his fingers trembling.

"That's enough, honey," she told him gently.

"No. Don't say that." She wasn't sure of his motivation, probably anger, but he shoved his hand under her dress roughly, hurting her and causing her to jump.

"I'm sorry." He took his hand away hastily.

"That's all right. You just got carried away."

"I couldn't help it. I love you so much."

"Let's get up, Charlie." It was getting late and she knew Dan would be angry with her.

"No." His protest was weak, uncertain.

"Charlie?"

Wordlessly, he got up from the chair, standing beside it and watching her as she stood in the center of the room.

"I'd better go. Thanks—for telling me."

"Don't go."

"Charlie, I've got to go. My husband's waiting for me at home. We have an invitation to a neighbor's house, and I have to be there."

"Don't go yet. Have another drink first. Please."

"I shouldn't—"

"You owe me that much."

She started to refuse again, then thought: What the hell, it was only another ten minutes or so, and if it would make him feel any better, then all right. She nodded to indicate her agreement, then walked to the window while he fixed the drinks, looking out on the street, the kids playing down the block, the police car cruising slowly by, the woman across the street sitting in front of their apartment building, getting the evening breeze as the sun started to dip out of sight.

They don't know how lucky they are, she told herself. Sitting out there, no problems, waiting for their husbands to come home from work. From the looks of them, dumpy, frowsy for the most part, they probably hadn't ever had to worry about adultery or the worse worry of being found out. She knew she could be wrong, but could temptation come with any regularity to people so obviously accustomed to their life and lot?

She thought not.

Charlie came back with the full glasses, and she drank hers quickly, wanting to feel the glow, wanting to be able to go home and act naturally, and not show the gnawing fear she felt at Joe's lack of discretion.

Charlie wasn't saying anything, just sipping at his drink and watching her.

Jane finished her drink, put the glass down on the coffee table. "Thanks again, Charlie. I'll have to hurry if I'm going to make that bus."

"Wait!" It was an order.

"What?"

"You're not leaving yet, not yet." His face was stern and grim, and his fists were clenched.

"I told you I had to leave after one more drink, Charlie," she said.

He walked toward her, and she saw the intenseness in him. "I asked you to go to bed with me, Jane. And you turned me down. Now I'm telling you."

Jane laughed lightly, trying to pass it off. "Honey, that's no way to get a girl interested in you."

"I mean it. Stop laughing!" He raised one hand and Jane flinched. But he didn't hit her. "Do you believe me now?"

She nodded. "I believe you, but—"

"You're going to go bed with me, or I'm going to tell your husband everything I heard Barton say today," he said, the words calm and even through his clenched teeth.

"Are you trying to blackmail me, Charlie?"

"Call it whatever you want to."

Jane faced him, wanting to feel anger at him, hatred for him, but couldn't. She felt a certain sympathy for him, plus the fondness she had always felt. And now, she admitted, a desire too, an awakened feeling that his new pose of masculinity had aroused.

And besides which, she told herself, what the hell difference does it make now? My reputation is shot. What harm would it do? And it might even be pretty good, she thought looking him up and down. He had the good solid build of an athletic young man, with still no signs of fat or paunch.

Besides, if I don't, he might really call Dan. Not that I hold out much hope any more for our beginning-again, but that would really blow it out.

She convinced herself that she had little choice, that it didn't matter anyway. But—oh that Joe Barton—was she going to have some choice words for *him* in the morning.

"All right," she said quietly, and smiled at the surprise in Charlie's face. "Didn't you think I would?"

"I—I didn't know."

They both waited, facing each other, until Jane remembered that young Charlie wouldn't know how to go about it. And she didn't want it to be messy—so she would have to show him.

"Come in here." She led the way into the bedroom. The mussed bed, the dirty clothes stacked in the corner could have been depressing, but she ignored them.

Standing beside the bed, she slipped off her dress quickly, then her slip. She sat on the edge of the bed and unfastened her stockings, rolling them down her smooth legs, dropping them with the other clothes. Then she turned to Charlie who was watching her with a trembling passion.

"Take off your clothes, Charlie."

"Okay." With fumbling hands, he removed everything but his underwear.

"Sit beside me."

"Okay."

Jane pushed him back on the bed by his shoulders, lying beside him, kissing him deeply and caressing him, rousing him to an even greater peak of excitement.

"Unfasten my bra," she told him.

"Okay," his words came through teeth chattering with nervousness and emotion. His hands fumbled, pulled, tugged, and finally he loosed the garment. Jane's breasts tumbled nakedly. His hands caught her.

Gradually, Jane felt her own desire building, overcoming her initial shock at the manner of his proposal, overcoming her own reluctance.

When they both were at a pitch where they could hardly stand it, she rolled away from him. "I want a cigarette."

"Not now, not now," he groaned, tugging at her last garment.

"Yes," she insisted. "Honest, Charlie, let's just take our time...."

"But—"

"Shhhh." Jane found her cigarettes and returned to the bed. They resumed their contact as they shared the cigarette. Jane chuckled when she saw the deep puffs Charlie would take in an effort to get it over with and get back to the business at hand.

"What's the rush?"

"Rush? After all these years, I'm gonna find out, and you wonder why I want to rush?" His voice squeaked.

"Take your time. It's better."

"Please hurry." He was the old Charlie again, the puppy-love, I-love-you Charlie, not the one who had angrily threatened blackmail if she persisted in leaving. He was the old Charlie and she knew she could do just about anything, the way he was.

Finally she put the cigarette out and turned back to him, renewing the building flame of passion, slowly working their way back to the peak they had avoided a few moments before. She found herself deliberately testing him, wondering how long it would take him to seize the initiative for himself.

Finally, Charlie was beyond a point of fearing he would do it wrong, and slipped his hand into her panties.

"That's right," she whispered as she caressed him.

Jane was amazed at his reaction. She stopped playing games then, afraid to persist in her teasing.

Rapidly she finished undressing herself, and then him. Then, very slowly, she helped him overcome his fear and insecurity and not-knowing. But he needn't have worried, not a bit, she thought. She pulled him tightly against herself.

She closed her eyes luxuriously and thought how much it was like swimming really—the body piercing the water, plunging deeply into the all-enveloping warmth of the water, then pulling up to the surface, gasping for air and diving down again—then at the ocean, where the breakers were biggest, letting one of them flood over you, smash into you with its tons of power and carry you along, willingly until it tossed you on the beach and you lay there on the hot sand, feeling completely drained and exhausted—and if you were alone you shouted out your glee.

Then you lay there for a long time.

"I love you," Charlie whispered, his breathing labored and heavy.

"You're sweet," she said, tousling his hair. "You don't have to ever worry again, Charlie—never never."

"I *was* worried."

"You shouldn't have been."

"I didn't know."

"You do now."

"Thanks to you. Look, I'm sorry about—the way I made you stay. Honest."

"Am I complaining?"

"No, but—"

"Look, baby, you may think I'm shameless, but I'd just be lying if I said I had any regrets. I don't. But I do hope you'll be more discreet than Barton."

He winced when she reminded him of that. "Don't worry, honey. I'll never tell anyone, never."

"I know you won't. Now I have to go home. Dan'll be ready to chew nails."

"Let me go with you. I can handle him."

Jane patted his face. "Thanks, Charlie, but that wouldn't make much sense really."

"I could tell him you were working late at the station and I drove you home."

"Uh uh. You don't know my husband like I do. It's better if I just take the bus, and face the music when I get there. All he can do is shout and yell and swear and pout, anyway." She eased herself off the bed, took a fast shower, then dressed while Charlie's adoring eyes watched her with a hunger to recapture the new-found rapture of a few minutes before.

"Jane?"

"I know what you're thinking, but the answer is no. I have *really* got to go home."

"When will you come again?"

She started to tell him never, started to answer him before she remembered that he didn't know of her plans, and thought over her words before she spoke. It would prove nothing to deny him any hope for another visit from her, and the only way to leave gracefully was to make him believe it would be soon. So she told him that.

"How soon?"

"I don't know, Charlie," she said, her voice muffled by her dress as she put it on again. "You just can't tell ahead of time— well, when will *be* a good time."

"Tomorrow?"

"No, I don't think so."

"Why not?"

"Look, Charlie, please don't force me. I told you—soon. And that's *all* I can tell you right now." Jane was ready to go, moved toward the door. Charlie, still naked, followed her.

"I'll see you at work tomorrow," he said.

"Yes. Now you get some clothes on, honey, before anyone comes. And before I get tempted to stay a little while longer," she added, not really meaning it but wanting to leave on a light note.

Charlie laughed. "Okay. Don't let it be too long, Janie. I want to see if I can do it again."

"Of course you can."

"I won't know 'til I try."

"Bye, Charlie." She closed the door to his apartment behind her and walked quickly down the stairs. It would be at least seven-thirty when she got home, and she began to worry immediately about Dan and what his reaction would be.

Jane felt that her debts were paid in full with Charlie, and that was worth the extra time it took. Barton was something else again. But tomorrow morning she would take care of him.

Her anger built up against him as she waited for her bus, as she rode home through the gathering dusk. Then, as she approached her stop, she put it out of her mind. She couldn't afford the luxury of thinking about something else when she greeted Dan. She hoped he'd had a few drinks, maybe even went ahead to the barbeque without her. That way, he wouldn't care so much that she was late, wouldn't be angry. And if that happened, then it was very possible that tonight could be the night that they started again.

She got off the bus and walked briskly down the familiar street toward her house. In the gloomy dusk, she saw the porch light on at their house, and Dan standing under it, waiting for her. Her nerves started tightening, anticipating what would come. Dan's impatience was apparent, even at a distance—a distance that narrowed with every step she took.

"Hi," she said, turning up the sidewalk to the house. Dan said nothing, just stood there with his hands on his hips, a scowl on his face.

"Sorry I'm late," she said.

"Where the hell have you been?" Dan stood blocking the door, and Jane didn't want to have a scene out front, where everyone could see.

"Let's go inside."

"I asked you a question."

"I'll tell you—but let's go inside," Jane repeated, her voice firmer. She pushed past him, knowing it would make him angrier, but determined to keep their problems to themselves as much as possible.

Dan followed her into the house, grabbing her arm and spinning her around to face him. "All right. Talk."

Jane watched his face for a moment, and almost decided to tell him exactly what *did* happen. But all she said was: "You sound like a policeman giving someone the third degree."

"That's not an answer."

"All right. After work—"

"Never mind."

"What?"

"I said 'never mind.' You probably have a jim-dandy story cooked up anyway. Just hurry up and get ready to go to the Andersons."

"Why didn't you go ahead by yourself, when I was late?"

"I should've, I guess."

"I guess there's no percentage in going over there alone when Stillwell's home," she said cattily, unable to resist it.

"Get ready," he said, his eyes blazing.

"*Si si, senor,*" Jane told him, and executed a little curtsey. "I weel be ready in a meenut."

"Very funny," Dan said dryly.

Jane hastened into the bedroom, changing her dress for shorts and a blouse. Dan came in and watched her, leaning in the doorway.

"Where *were* you anyway?" he asked when she was ready.

"Why, Danny Boy, I was shacked up with one of the announcers," she told him lightly, daring him to believe it.

"In other words, it's none of my business?"

"I just told you."

"Okay. You're quite the *comedienne* tonight," he said, his face downcast and sullen.

"I've got a million of 'em."

"Are you ready?"

"Just."

"Then let's go, dammit."

"Yes, *sir.*" She was trying to keep it light, flippant. This type of thing made him sullen, but it was better than butting heads with him.

They were the last ones at the barbeque. Harry and Alice had preceeded them by quite some time, they learned later. When they walked up, the ham was sizzling on the spit as the pungent smoke of the juices dropping on the red-hot coals billowed around it, before swirling into the night air.

"Smells good," Jane called. She and Dan were greeted with shouts.

"Thought you weren't coming."

"We were just gonna come look for you."

"Yeah, thought maybe you fell in again, Janie," followed by Harry's raucous laughter. Jane accepted a drink from Harry. She could use one. Looking around she saw that Dan had already landed beside Marilyn. The blonde wore the skimpiest of shorts, with a halter that had been made for someone at least four sizes smaller in the bust. She was proving again that Nature had endowed her generously, and Dan was enjoying every bit of it.

Jane walked over to the pit where Still was tending the preparation of the meal. "Sorry we're late."

"Think nothing of it. You're in time to eat and that's what really counts."

"You're right, from the aroma. There's nothing like outdoor cooking."

Stillwell stood up, glancing over at Dan and his wife. "Unless it's outdoor parlor games, huh?" chuckling quietly. Jane noticed he was weaving a little, and realized he had been drinking more heavily than usual. She decided she'd better get his mind off Marilyn and Dan.

"Oh, that," with an offhand wave. "I think our mates are just having a little trouble growing up all the way, Still. But I'm not at all worried about it."

"You're not?"

"No. It doesn't amount to a hill of beans. It's when stuff like that goes undercover, that we have to worry, Out here in plain sight—what's to worry about?"

"I don't know, Jane." He turned to her, his eyes holding hers with a starkness she hadn't seen before. "Just keep Dan away from Marilyn, huh?"

"Oh sure, Still—" she began, but he interrupted her.

"I mean it, Jane. Keep him away."

"Okay," she said soberly, surprised by the seriousness of his manner. "Okay," she repeated, nodding slightly.

"Now grab a plate and let's eat," he said, smiling again, and Jane was relieved. But she pondered his words as she ate the delicious supper.

A fat lot of good *I* can do, she told herself. If I tell Dan to stay away from Marilyn, that'll just drive him to her every chance he gets.

Harry Gordon sat beside her. "How you been?"

"All right."

"Good." He grinned self-assuredly. "Glad to hear it." He kept staring at her, and Jane found herself becoming annoyed.

"Eat your supper," she said.

"Sure, baby. I make you nervous?"

"No."

"I shouldn't. We know each other pretty well, don't we?" he asked, whispering.

"Well enough."

"Maybe we'll know each other better, one of these days."

"I doubt it."

"Aw, c'mon now."

"Listen Harry, you apparently don't remember things very clearly. But I do. And one thing you're not," she told him through clenched teeth, "one thing you are *definitely not*—is a great lover."

Harry blinked, slowly comprehending what she had said. Then he blushed and averted his eyes. He got up without another word and joined Alice, who was with Dan and Marilyn. Jane walked over to Stillwell, pleased with herself for putting Harry in his place. She didn't think she'd be having any more trouble with him.

"You're to be complimented, Still."

"Thanks," he said unsmiling.

"That ham was extra special."

"I soaked it in a secret formula all night."

"You'll have to tell me about it."

"Sure. I will, sometime." He was talking to her, but his eyes kept going to his wife. Marilyn was feeling her drinks and swayed her body in time with music that was being piped out to the patio from the Anderson's hi-fi set. As she swayed, she bumped into Dan frequently, brushing him with her almost naked breasts or her full hips. Every once in awhile Dan would put his hand on Marilyn's bare back as he said something to her, and Jane knew he was touching her more than necessary.

Ordinarily, she would have just said to hell with it, and forgotten it—but tonight Still kept watching them with murky, brooding eyes.

Finally, she couldn't take anymore of Dan's pawing, and made her excuses. Alice and Still asked her to stay, Harry even acted disappointed in a half-hearted manner, Marilyn said the evening was young—but Dan said nothing, nor did he come back to the house with her.

Jane undressed rapidly, then put on her shorty pajamas for the warm night. The bed felt good. She was tired from the long day and went quickly to sleep, the sounds of the party next door dimly registering briefly.

Jane was rudely awakened by Dan, in bed with her, his hands on her breasts tightly.

"Why didn't you wait for me?" he demanded, his breath foul with liquor.

"I was tired. I still am, Dan."

He pushed her back on her pillow. His hands went under her pajama top, then worked the brief panties off her body.

"I'm tired, I said."

"Be quiet," he told her.

Jane did as he directed, still groggy from sleep. She knew what was happening, knew that Marilyn had aroused him to a point where he had to have her to let off steam.

Why fight it? she thought. It's almost over with already.

Then it was over.

Dan stumbled over to his bed, falling on it. He was sound asleep and snoring when Jane returned. She stood beside his bed a moment, staring angrily down at him.

That's the last time you're gonna get hot with that bitch then come home to me, she thought. The last time!

And tonight we were going to start again. Ha!

Maybe we have, she told herself. Maybe this is what's going to be, from now on. Maybe I've had my beginning-again and didn't even know it.

The thought was bitter, yet she couldn't completely dismiss it.

Maybe this is it. Wouldn't *that* be something?

CHAPTER THIRTEEN

ONLY ONE thing was on Jane's mind as she rode the bus to work the next morning:

Joe Barton and his big mouth!

The more she thought about it, the angrier she became, so that by the time she was in her office, she was in fine fettle.

But Barton wasn't in yet, and she sat fuming at her desk as she waited. A few calls came in which she handled with dispatch, but she made no attempt to open the mail or take care of any of her other duties.

He walked in at nine-thirty, nodded to her, and went into his office.

Jane got up and followed him, slamming the door shut behind them. Barton turned with surprise.

"Do you have to be that noisy?"

"Yes."

"What's on your mind?" he asked, sensing her mood.

"I understand you've been talking about me."

"Meaning what?" He was acting innocently, but a wariness was in his manner.

"Don't play games with me, Joe."

"I don't know what you're talking about," he protested, going behind his desk and sitting down. "Now, if you've got something to say, spit it out."

"All right. I think you're a son of a bitch, a dirty, sneaky bastard!"

"Now just a damn minute!" he said, standing again.

"You told me to say it. I did."

"What brought that on?"

"You! You've been telling people about our trip to New York. I never expected that of *you,* Joe, but then I guess I didn't know what a bastard you are."

"Where did you hear that?"

"Does it matter?"

"But it's not the truth, Janie. I swear it." He was putting on a good act, but Jane decided it was time to puncture his balloon of lies.

"You swear it, huh?"

"Yes."

"You haven't told anyone?"

"No. No one."

"You lie so well, Joe. If I didn't know better, I'd almost believe you. But I know you told someone—one anyway—all about our trip, and everything that happened on it. And I mean *everything.*"

"Whoever told you that lied!"

"Did they lie about my mole, too?" she asked quietly.

"Mole—?"

"Yes, Joe. My mole. M … O … L … E."

"Oh!" Barton realized she knew the truth. For a moment, he paled, then another thought took hold of him. "Well, it wouldn't have happened if you'd been more cooperative yesterday. You made me pretty mad, Janie. Maybe that'll be a lesson to you."

"Joe, there are two things I can't stand. Slimy little things like roaches and rats and snakes—and men who kiss and tell. I really can't see any difference between one and the other. And one more thing," she said, feeling better every minute. "If you don't keep your mouth shut about me and that trip, I'll throw that mole in your wife's face—and I'll give her an earful. If you think the story of what really happened is a hot one, wait'll you hear the one I'll tell *her.*"

Joe paled again. "You wouldn't do that, Janie," he said weakly.

"Don't you bet on it, buster. One more word about me, and that's *just* what I'll do. And if you think I'm kidding—you just try me."

"Look, I'm sorry, honey. Honest. I'll tell—well, I'll tell the guy I told that I was just lying. Okay? And that'll be the end of it. But keep the wife out of it. Okay?"

"Just remember what I told you, Joe Barton."

"I will, I will."

Jane started back to her office. At the door, she paused and faced him again. "One more thing, Joe."

"Yes?"

"I quit."

"What?"

"You heard me."

"You can't do that."

"Wanna bet?"

"But—I *need* you. Hell, Janie, I don't know where a damn thing is here. You got to work at least until you can train someone." He was pleading with her, and she studied him before she said the next words.

"You can take this job and you know what you can do with it, boy. Just remember what I said about your wife." Jane went quickly out the door and slammed it hard. She picked up her purse from the desk, walked out of the office, out of the station.

She debated going to an early movie, but decided against it. Now that she was truly a housewife, she wanted to get home and fix things up. Her working had bothered Dan—but perhaps now, with that out of the way, things could be better.

As she approached her house, she saw with surprise that Dan's car was still there. She knew he was planning to work locally, but he should have started long ago. He'd been awake when she left earlier, taking a shower and fighting a hangover.

Jane let herself in the house quietly, listening for a sound that would indicate Dan's location. At first, she heard nothing—then there was a slight noise from the bedroom.

She smiled, started tiptoeing toward the room.

A woman giggled.

Jane stopped, the chills of shock and surprise racing through her. She listened carefully, immobile, and heard it again. A half-smothered giggle, then a slap of a hand on bare flesh.

She waited a moment, realizing that she felt no anger. Even the surprise was gone. It was as though she had expected to come home to this someday, and the day had finally come.

Jane slipped off her shoes, walked silently to the bedroom doorway. Peering in, she saw a lush naked leg stretching in the air, parts of the woman's body, all of Dan's. There was no doubt the woman was Marilyn, even though Jane couldn't see her face.

The two of them were concentrating on their own activities and had no awareness of her.

"Oh Danny, that's good," Marilyn said.

Jane chuckled to herself at her timing. Another few minutes and—

"Hurry," Dan said to her.

"I am, I am," she whispered back.

Jane decided that it was time to make her presence known.

"What's the hurry?" she asked loudly.

The two bodies on the bed stopped immediately. Dan whirled around, seeing her, his face blanching, all color draining from it. Marilyn pushed herself up on her elbows, emitting a tiny scream when she saw Jane standing there in the doorway.

"This isn't what you think, Jane," Dan said stupidly, jumping off the bed and drawing on his trousers.

"Of course not," Jane commented dryly.

"Nothing's happened, Jane," Marilyn said, pulling a sheet up to her shoulders, her eyes wide with fear.

"I know. I've been watching."

"Oh."

"Put your clothes on, Marilyn, and get out of here, please."

"Sure." The blonde slipped out of bed, donning her garments hastily. Jane studied her body, the ripeness of it, and saw how it could drive men to thoughts of possessing it. Not that I don't have a good body myself, she thought. Marilyn's just got a little more of everything.

When Marilyn was dressed, she turned to Jane as though she wanted to say something, but Jane held up her hand.

"Don't say a word. It's not necessary."

"But—"

"Leave—now."

"All right." Marilyn went quickly out of the room. Jane listened until she heard the kitchen door shut, then she turned to Dan. He stood beside the bed, not meeting her eyes.

"Was it worth it?" she asked quietly.

"There's nothing I can say. She came over, took her clothes off, practically was raping me." Dan shrugged. "I—I just couldn't help myself."

"I think you could have been more careful. You know what they say about having affairs with people you work with or people who live near you. Very bad taste." She waited for him to say something, but he was staring hard at his feet and made no move to speak. "I'm *not* mad, Dan."

He looked up then, startled. "You're *not?*"

"No." She was really almost grateful. Finding him as she had helped ease her own guilt.

"I don't get it." His confusion was evident.

"I'm not sure I can explain it—but I'm going to try." Jane sat on the edge of the bed. "I want you to listen to me and listen good. When I'm all through, then you say your piece, but don't interrupt me until—"

The sound of a loud explosion ripped through the house, silencing her words.

"What was that?" Dan asked.

Jane felt her insides turning to jelly. "I hope it's not what I'm afraid it is." She jumped up from the bed, raced to a window that overlooked the Anderson's yard. A gasp escaped her lips as she saw Marilyn lying in the driveway, her dress above her knees. Stillwell stood over her, a pistol in his hand still smoking. "Oh, God," Jane muttered. "Oh, God!"

Dan stood beside her, his face again ashen. Stillwell looked over at their house, and Dan fell to the floor. "He's gonna come over here. He's crazy. He's gonna come over here and shoot me," Dan said, terrified.

"I don't think so," Jane told him calmly. "He's just looking. Now he's looking down at Marilyn again." She made her decision "I'm going out there."

"You *can't*. He might shoot you, too."

"I don't think so." She started to leave, but Dan held her dress tightly. "Let go, Dan."

"Don't go. Don't. Don't leave me here alone." He started to cry, and Jane disentangled herself abruptly. "Please, Jane," he pleaded, but she ignored him and went outside the house.

Stillwell saw her coming, pointed the gun at her. "Don't come any closer, Jane."

"Why'd you do it, Still?"

"Had to. Just like you shoot a mad dog." He laughed sadly. "I made her tell me where she'd been. Well, she won't be making trips to anyone else's bedroom." He looked down at his wife's body, and tears came into his eyes. "I guess she was just too much for me." He shook his head slowly.

Far away, Jane heard a siren screaming and knew the police were on the way. "Still?"

"What?"

"Put the gun down. I'm not going to move. But put it down before the police come."

Stillwell shook his head.

"If they come and see you standing there with a gun, they might shoot first, *then* ask what's going on."

Stillwell only shook his head again. The sound of the sirens came closer, and in a moment, a patrol car squealed

Two policemen got out of their car warily drawing their guns.

"He's all right," Jane called to them. "Don't shoot him."

The cops walked up to Stillwell, taking his gun without any difficulty. One of them bent down beside Marilyn.

"Who is this?" he asked Stillwell, pointing to Marilyn's body.

"That *was* my wife. My wife and everybody's pleasure," Still answered in an undertone. "I killed her. She said she was going to leave me. So I killed her. It's as simple as that, officer. Shall we go downtown?"

The policeman turned to Jane. "Did you witness this?"

"No. I heard the shot and ran out. I saw the same thing you did when you drove up."

"She doesn't know anything about it," Stillwell told him. "Like I said, Marilyn was leaving me. I told her not to. When she persisted, I shot her."

The policemen handcuffed Still and led him to the police car, ushering him into the back seat. One remained with him, while the other called in on their radio. Presently, more police arrived, then an ambulance, a photographer and reporters.

Jane told the policeman that she wasn't aware of any trouble between the Andersons. He made notes, then told her she could leave.

The reporters besieged her.

"I don't know anything," Jane told them. "There's been a shooting, that's all I know."

They kept after her while she walked back to her house. At the door, she turned to them. "Please. Those people were friends of mine. I'm quite upset. Please leave me alone."

Jane let herself in the house wearily. Dan hastened to her. "What's happening? What did Still say? Did he tell 'em what happened?" Dan was frightened and shocked.

"Still told them nothing. He's going to take all the blame for it, from what he said. It doesn't seem fair really, but that's apparently what he wants."

"Not *fair*? Hell, Jane, *he* shot her. We didn't." Dan took a deep breath, regaining his composure once he had digested the news that he wouldn't be involved in the unpleasantness, the publicity, the scandal.

"He shot her because she was over *here*—in bed with *you*, Dan. And you know it. If he wants to ignore that, then that's *his* business."

"Even if he said anything, we could deny it. He couldn't prove a thing. We could just say he was crazy jealous all the time. Marilyn just came over here to borrow something. We could even—"

"SHUT UP!"

"Jane?"

"Shut up! Sometimes Dan, you're the most spineless sonuvabitch I've ever seen. You disgust me when you act like that."

"What do you mean?"

"Just this. To a degree, you're to blame for Marilyn's death. If Still keeps you out of it, be thankful. But if he brings you in, buster, you're going to own up to it. Because that's what a *man* would do—and you're going to start acting like one. Beginning right now!"

"Do you think he'll involve me?"

"No, I don't."

"I wish it had never happened."

"I'm sure you do. I'm sure we all do, including Marilyn. But it *did* happen. And nothing will erase that." Jane took a deep breath. There was more to be said, and she felt there was no better time than right then.

"Let's get a few things straight, Dan'l. I wasn't angry when I came home and found you in bed with Marilyn. I wasn't angry for one good reason. You're not the only one in this family who can play around."

"You're going to—?"

"Not 'going to.' Have."

"With who?"

"*That* is none of your business, my friend. But it's enough for you to know that I have. And I know *you* have. So we're even. If you're willing, that's as good a place to start as any."

"Start?"

"Yes. I quit my job today."

"Why?"

"Again, that's not important. But it presents a possibility. I'm willing to be a housewife, and only a housewife, if you're willing to settle down and be a husband—to me alone. No playing patsy when you're on trips, no feeling other men's wives. No more heavy drinking. And you'll have to buckle down and make more money, since I won't be working. At least that's what I had in mind when I quit."

"I'll do it, Janie. Honest. Just give me the chance."

"I mean it, Dan. If you slip just once, I'll walk out on you and that'll be the end of it. I know myself, and I know *I* can do it. I'm not sure about you."

"Just give me the chance," he begged. "I've learned a lesson today. I don't think I'll forget it in a hurry either. You can believe that!" He was sweating with the intensity of his plea, and Jane found herself convinced that he meant it.

"All right," she said, and smiled gently at him. "I believe you. And I do want us to start again. We had something pretty good once. Maybe we can get it back."

"If tryin' will do it ... "

"You wait here."

"Why?"

"You'll see." Jane went into the bedroom and closed the door. From her dresser she pulled forth the diaphanous nightgown she had bought in New York for the beginning-again. Slowly she undressed, her emotions torn between happiness that they were finally going to start, both knowing what the past held, both knowing only they themselves could keep the future right, torn between that and sadness over Marilyn.

Jane removed the last of her garments, then powdered her body generously, admiring her high pointed breasts in the mirror, her flat stomach. Then she put on the nightgown, throwing the wrapping to the floor. The gown, its newness, made her feel new too, new and fresh and unspoiled. It hid nothing, only added the tantalizing touch that she knew Dan liked.

I'm ready, she thought, and started for the door, when the phone rang. She heard Dan answer it.

"Jane?"

"What is it?"

"It's for you."

Jane came out of the bedroom, standing poised in the doorway for a moment, letting her husband savor the sight that greeted his eyes. His mouth fell open with surprise. Jane walked to the phone, knowing Dan was watching her, knowing he took delight in what he saw.

"Yes?" she said into the receiver.

"Janie. This is Charlie."

"What is it please?"

"I just found out you quit."

"That's right."

"Why?"

Jane turned so that she faced Dan. She smiled at him before answering Charlie. "A number of reasons."

"Look, I want to see you. I've got to talk to you, honey."

"I'm busy right now. In fact, I think I'm going to be busy from now on."

Dan had moved closer to her, and his hands were caressing her body tenderly. Jane felt the tingling begin.

"Jane, this is Charlie, remember. If you don't come see me this afternoon, I'll have to tell your husband about that trip," Charlie said, and Jane sensed the frustration and anger that he felt.

"He knows all about it," she said, pressing herself against Dan as he pulled her close against his body. "Look, why don't you find yourself a nice young girl your own age? You'd really be better off."

Dan grinned at her words, thumbing his nose at the phone. His hands never stopped caressing her, and Jane knew it was time for other things.

"Janie? Please, baby?" Charlie pleaded.

"No. We had our fun, young 'un. But it's over. Understand?" Jane hung up the phone abruptly and threw herself at her husband, clinging to him as tightly as she could. "I'm sorry for the delay," she told Dan. "I had to brush off an old flame."

"Think nothing of it," he said, smiling. "There's no hurry." So saying, he picked her up in his arms and carried her to the living room divan. He laid her down easily, then joined her, kissing her with a building passion.

"If you're going to be a housewife," he told her between kisses, "you'll have to put up with a lot of this."

"I think I'm able," she whispered, nibbling his ear. "Just try me."

"Yes, ma'am."

Jane closed her eyes, enjoying the prelude to love. Dan was taking his time and she felt like purring. It had been a long time since he'd been this good, this careful. She helped him remove the gown, then lay back again and made a silent vow.

I'll be true as long as he is, she told herself. As long as he's as sweet as this, as long as he remembers to be considerate and kind, as long as he's a good husband, I'll be a good wife, I swear.

And if he slips—well, there's always Charlie, young and hot and eager.

But Dan showed no signs of slipping. His lips were awakening responses that she had never known, and she moaned with delight.

It was going to be good, she thought. Life was going to be good, like it used to be.

She thought about Harry briefly. He wouldn't make any more trouble. She'd found that out at the barbeque, when she'd reminded him of how unsatisfactory he'd been. No, Harry might stray, but not into her pasture, not again.

And Dan—she couldn't believe it, the way he was making her feel. It was like—like the days when they'd first been married, when they'd spent all their time devising pleasures for each other, unhurried, leisurely.

"Oh Danny boy, that's enough. I can't stand any more."

"Try," he whispered.

"I feel like I'm going to burst if you don't do something quick!" Dan's eyes met hers. "I love you," he said simply.

"Oh, I love you too, Danny. I always have."

"We won't get off the track again, baby."

"I hope not."

"I promise, baby."

"Me too. Now get busy and put me out of my misery, my friend. Before I start screaming."

"Okay."

Later, she did scream.

Not loud.

Just for Dan to hear.

THE END